WITHDRAWN

Sandrine Collette was born in Paris in 1970. She divides her time between Nanterre, where she teaches philosophy and literature, and Burgundy, where she has a horse stud farm. She is the author of numerous novels, including *Nothing but Dust* (Europa, 2018), winner of the Landerneau Prize for crime fiction, and *Just after the Wave* (Europa, 2020).

Alison Anderson's translations for Europa Editions include novels by Sélim Nassib, Amélie Nothomb, and Eric-Emmanuel Schmitt. She is the translator of Muriel Barbery's *The Elegance of the Hedgehog*.

ALSO BY

SANDRINE COLLETTE

Nothing but Dust
Just after the Wave

THE FORESTS

Sandrine Collette

THE FORESTS

*Translated from the French
by Alison Anderson*

Europa
editions

Europa Editions
1 Penn Plaza, Suite 6282
New York, N.Y. 10019
www.europaeditions.com
info@europaeditions.com

Translation by Alison Anderson
Original title: *Et toujours les Forêts*
Translation copyright © 2022 by Europa Editions

Library of Congress Cataloging in Publication Data is available
ISBN 978-1-60945-729-7

Collette, Sandrine
The Forests

Book design by Emanuele Ragnisco
www.mekkanografici.com

Cover illustration by Ginevra Rapisardi

Prepress by Grafica Punto Print – Rome

Printed in Italy

The first angel sounded, and there followed hail
and fire mingled with blood,
and they were cast upon the earth:
and the third part of trees was burnt up,
and all green grass was burnt up.
—REVELATION 8:7

THE FORESTS

The old women had said as much, they who saw everything: a life that had begun in such a way could not come to anything good.

The old women did not know then how right they were, nor what this little life growing where no life was wanted would come to know in the way of disaster and misfortune. And far beyond that life itself: it was the world that would collapse. But no one knew that yet.

At that moment, it was impossible to foresee.

At that moment, these were merely the mutterings of old women, and it was only the next day, and the day after, that mattered to them, and what people would say, because the village rustled and whispered and throbbed with rumors, constantly speaking. And because they had sensed the ill wind, they had decided to block their ears, to seal their lips, in the end, as if that might suffice. It was basically not much to worry about, not the sort of thing that warranted lengthy discussion.

And besides, by the time the true, great chaos arrived, the old women would probably not be there anymore to talk about it.

But in the meantime, it was there.

It was there, clinging deep inside, to Marie's womb. The way you might refer to a farm animal, a cow or a ewe or a mare, it had taken hold. By chance, perhaps, by mischance, surely, in any event it was there now, and she would have to reckon with it.

Marie did not even know where it came from.
That cursed little life.

* * *

Marie, holding her large belly in her hands, her hair sticky with sweat despite the cool night air.

Marie who didn't even think about it anymore, this thing growing in her gut; just now, she was too terrified of the Forests. Because the old women had known exactly what they were doing: they left her there, amid the gloom and the trees, exactly halfway between the day before and the day after.

They left her there, they'd opened the door of the derelict house buried in the dark wood, and they'd shoved her toward the threshold. Outside, you couldn't see a thing. A night as dark as ink. A night for ogres. And they'd said, "Out you go!"

That door, opened for the first time in six months.

Marie had looked at the old women, Alice and Augustine, the way you would look at madwomen. Marc's and Jérémie's grandmothers. A race of dogs and lunatics, every last one.

But Marie didn't understand anymore. She was frightened.
And then there was her belly, so round and heavy.
She shook her head, imploring.
Where was she supposed to go.
What did they care, the old women.

Six months locked away in a shuttered room, and now Marie was regaining her freedom in the middle of the night, along with the twenty or thirty pounds from the child to come: Marie, who had retreated into the room.

And so, the grannies had driven her out, waving their brooms, until they could close the door behind her.

Until Marie was far away, because she knew this: that door would only ever open again to let in misfortune.

There was no moon that night.

Marie could hardly even see the narrow road she went down in a daze. Sometimes she stumbled in the grass or on brambles and fell to her knees. She got up, sobbing, one hand scratched by nettles, the other on the still-warm asphalt. She ran both hands under her belly and hoisted herself back to her feet, once again trembling. Once again blind.

No cars went by, for hours.

Just the trees, with their huge branches flung out like dislocated arms, and the wind making strange sounds: rustling, murmuring, threatening.

Just the looming outline of beech and chestnut trees above her, closing over in an impenetrable vault, their roots like snares, their birds and insects aroused by her tears to brush against her and fly away in a whir of discontent.

Just the Forests.

* * *

The Forests had never liked Marie.
They weren't about to guide her.
They weren't about to help her.

* * *

Marie didn't like them either. What she liked was the city—the lights, the never-ending party. When she'd met Jérémie, she'd torn him away from this damp, spellbinding territory she hated. She had pretended to ignore the hold the Forests had over the people who were born there. She thought it was just old wives' tales. It was nothing compared to what she wanted, her promises, her hair streaming in the wind.

The Forests: a land of men and old women.

That there might not be room for her there, she didn't care. She'd leave.

But not on her own.

And so, she'd taken Jérémie with her.

She had parted him from his land and his friends, from his grandmother Alice, from his past. She didn't give a damn.

And she was convinced she'd put that place behind them. She believed you could tell fate what to do, that sodden earth doesn't necessarily stick to the soles of your shoes. She made Jérémie swear never to set foot there again—and he had sworn.

And then.

One day he went back, on leave, for a weekend. And finally, forever. The Forests had called him back, the way you whistle to your dog. He'd come running, tongue hanging out, eyes aglow.

Maybe that was what Marie had never forgiven him for.

She was even sure of it.

Those accursed Forests.

* * *

Marie went on walking through the trees. Sometimes she turned around, as if the old women might have come after her to take her back, and she shivered with fear. She could hear her breathing, hoarse in her throat and in her head.

Anything other than the rustling of these dark woods.

Her belly hurt.

She banged her fist against the taut skin.

Just stop it.

She hated this bump that was part of her and, in vain, she'd tried to get rid of this excrescence that would only go away once she gave birth, because of Alice and Augustine, the grandmothers of those worthless grandsons, who had sequestered her for six months.

You don't mean you'll actually do it? Fuck, you don't mean it?

Six months.

In the early days of her confinement, Marie had rammed the walls of the room, belly first, to hit it all the harder, to make the child go away. She pictured it as a sort of squirrel perched on her organs, and which a slightly harder blow, maybe sideways, would eventually knock off. But the baby boy—since it would turn out to be a boy—had clung on like the wind to a fragile branch. After a few weeks Marie had to concede defeat, and she began to count the terrible days: the baby would be born, she had lost all hope.

Marie was imprisoned, shut away in a dark room, for everything she had ruined, broken, destroyed by going to parade her ass elsewhere. They would teach her a lesson, destroy her life the way she'd destroyed Marc's and Jérémie's—that's what they said.

Jérémie and Marc, like two fingers of the same hand, before.

Before Marie.

The girl who had the whole village talking—twenty-odd hicks glued to her story, the scandal of it.

Woe betide she who brings misfortune.

* * *

Terrified by the darkness of the Forests, by the unfamiliar sounds in the air, the invisible creatures: she tried to cheer herself on, speaking in a quiet voice.

The night was never-ending. Her legs didn't want to carry her anymore, didn't want to walk. Her eyes bulged, looking out for a car. A light. Someone.

Her big belly, too heavy.

* * *

Of course, she had been in love with Jérémie in the beginning. She only had eyes for him. They married. Too hastily. A year went by, then two, and a third. The time seemed long. She wanted so badly to have fun.

Have fun? Not even.

The actual word was: to live.

Jérémie was like a little dog. He was always there. Marie tired of him.

In the summer, he broke his promise, and they were both back in the Forests. Then before long, to banish boredom, there were three of them: there was Marc, Jérémie's childhood friend.

At the boys' grandmothers—the old bitches, Marie amended, in silence.

All right, when Jérémie went back to work at the end of the vacation, she did sleep with Marc. It went on for two or three months. A lovely late summer. Jérémie came on weekends, he said Marie needed to rest, needed to have fun. Well, she'd found some entertainment.

So, had it been such a bad thing, had it been worth all the shouting, the blows, the lives torn apart; the fight that had left Jérémie and Marc breathless and bloodied and on bad terms for life.

Jérémie had slammed the car door and driven off like a madman. He'd left Marie behind with old Alice. Marie wasn't worried. She knew he'd be back the next day, tail between his legs. She expected him to apologize. She prepared her own explanation, because there would have to be one. It took her half the night, but she would never have the opportunity to give it, because Jérémie didn't come back.

He was killed that night, on the road. A bad bend, where those huge plane trees stood, unforgiving. Such bad luck.

It was her fault—screamed Alice, outside the bedroom door.

* * *

Marie could think of only one thing: how to get out of there.

She'd only just found out she was pregnant. She had to get an abortion.

Marc didn't answer any of her calls. Later she would find out that he had left the Forests when he heard about Jérémie's death. Where had he gone? Even his grandmother didn't know. All he'd said was that it would be for good.

Marie didn't really care. She didn't wonder who'd planted the nasty thing that was suddenly growing in her belly.

It didn't matter.

She just wanted to be rid of it.

Good and rid.

If the grandmothers hadn't been there to stop her.

Shouting at her through the locked door that she'd be keeping the kid right to the end, that it would be there all her life to remind her.

* * *

Marie dragged herself through the night and couldn't stop crying. Eventually she wasn't even afraid of the Forests anymore, she hadn't the strength.

It was the end of summer, the air was warm.

In another time, she would have thought it was fun to be walking through the dark, holding Jérémie's hand—or Marc's, either one, for all the difference it made. They would've opened their palms to the breeze, they would've listened to the owl hooting, even if Marie didn't care, they would've raced through the dark. They would've made up names for the shapes of the giant trees, names they alone knew, for a world that belonged to them alone.

All of that had been smashed to pieces.

She was running away from the Forests, her belly hurt, she had to stop hitting it. She just had to keep on walking, ever farther. And find a car that would take her to town. After that, she didn't know. After was too far away. With too many questions.

Because what would it be like, life, afterwards—what would it be like, being a mother, murmured a little voice inside, but no way, anything but that, the old women were not about to win, she swore they wouldn't. She was not going to love it, the brat, she'd dump it somewhere and she'd go and conquer her own paradise, her dream life, she deserved it, she'd paid up front. Basically, a child could be erased, like a chalk line on a blackboard. All you needed was a good rag.

She could never figure out why she hadn't simply abandoned him at birth. She'd spend the rest of her life regretting the fact.

Something had stopped her.

Maybe it was the immense solitude.

Maybe it was her refusal to accept that somewhere else the child might be loved, and have a good life. And she didn't want him to be happy.

As a result, every time he would try to be happy, Marie would go to any length to destroy the world he'd invented.

* * *

She had no family. She had a few girlfriends and, after she gave birth, she left the little boy with them, one after the other. The time to catch her breath. The time to work. And the time to get an earful, so she'd come back for him, because it wasn't normal—forgetting a child for weeks on end, sometimes months, disappearing, impossible to reach, this conviction of Marie's that other people might as well end up raising her child with their own kids.

The little boy was shunted around from one house to the next, his eyes wide open, looking at everything. He never made a sound, he didn't cry, he wasn't a babbly baby. Occasionally he recognized Marie's voice when she showed up after a long absence, when she was arguing with her girlfriends. It always ended in tears, and afterwards, she'd settle him in the car and slam the door and shout, *You're a fucking pain in the ass!*

For a few days or weeks, he'd be back in the tiny, poorly lit apartment where his mother lived. She left him on his own, she had to earn a living, after all. He could cry for hours: no one ever came, no one ever responded to his cries. He gazed at the carpet, distraught. With his finger he traced the pictures, the colors. His gaze faltered. The afternoons were too long. He eventually fell asleep.

When Marie came home, he held out his hands to her when he heard her opening the door. She didn't look at him.

* * *

Corentin turned two, then three.

What am I going to do with you.

Through the half open door, inside the car, he remained silent. He knew it was all his fault. Misfortune was his lot, his mother said as much as she leaned over him.

All you ever bring me is bad luck.

That Marie herself might be the problem—there was no one to explain this to him. Her moodiness, her impossible desires. She was so pretty that men were taken in; and then came the rages, the capriciousness, the demands. By the time they met Corentin, they'd already been looking for a way out of the impossible relationship for a long time. And even so, the little boy nearly made them think twice about escape, he was that touching in his little blue trousers, doing his best to keep up with the grown-ups, to follow them without making a sound, to be satisfied with the most insignificant little things.

But Marie.

Her extravagance always got the better of them.

Who wants a woman with a kid? she'd shout afterwards, pointing at him.

Corentin stood there next to her, silent, his big eyes terrified and steeped with an impossible love.

Wait for it to pass.

As long as his mother was there, something existed.

She who dreamt of being able to abandon him somewhere. Yes, with all her strength, she wanted to make him disappear. Sometimes when her reason failed her, she would look for a way out, a magic wand. There were times it kept her awake at night, she'd place the wand on the boy's head and he would dissolve into the air, nothing left, just a puff of smoke and a huge, incredible feeling of freedom.

Seized with an insane hope, Marie went to look in the alcove where she made him sleep between two chancy stints at a babysitter's. He was still there.

Still fucking there.

* * *

One day, it had been almost five years.

One day it had been eighteen months since Marie dumped him on Olive, in return for his board, cash. To improve Olive's everyday fare, because bringing up three kids all on your own, she said to Marie, who wasn't listening, is hard. No matter how much she worked, cleaning people's houses, cooking for them, ironing; no matter how much, even with what she got from the state, it didn't go very far. So another banknote or two was always welcome.

When she got it.

It drove Marie crazy to have to pay for the brat. She showed up once every three months, and Olive told her off. Did she think her son only ate one month out of the three?

Marie tossed the money on the table, lowered her voice slightly, and Corentin was out of her hands for another few months.

And Marie was out: she didn't show up anymore, until Olive's frantic calls obliged her to, because the so-called letters containing the cash for the boy's keep had never arrived.

* * *

So, of course, he found out his mother was paying for him to stay there. It took him a week to get over it.

Corentin would never have believed it—Corentin thought Olive loved him.

So this was what life was about: you paid for someone to love you.

Her kids—Jojo, two years older than him, and the two little girls, Anaïs and Manon—had taken him outside to play. They ran together through the forest that didn't really look like a forest: it was still too close to the Big City. But even if it wasn't the countryside, it wasn't the city anymore either: a sort of in-between of scattered concrete surrounded by trees and fake ponds, to look as if.

They lay down by the greenish pond on the far side of the little grove with the fishing rods a neighbor had made for them. They caught some roach that they threw back (in the beginning, they brought them home, and Olive cooked them, nothing must go to waste, but the white flesh had a disgusting silty smell; after that they stopped bringing them home, and just said they weren't biting anymore).

They gazed at the sky and the clouds while they waited for the fish to bite. This time Corentin looked at the other three with new eyes. He realized now that he didn't belong to their world. He wasn't one of them—they didn't have the same mother, they weren't the same family.

They all acted as if.

But it wasn't true.

The hurt stayed deep inside him for a while. And then one

day, Corentin stopped thinking about it. He was almost happy. As the months went by, he stopped missing his mother so badly. Even if Olive was strict, it didn't stop the four kids from roaming the outdoors, wading in the pond, hiding in the hut, then stuffing themselves on the pasta or potatoes that were on the menu every evening.

When it was the season, Corentin went off with Jojo into the woods and along the trails to pick berries: wild raspberries, blueberries, blackberries. Olive made delicious pies. All summer long they hunted for porcini and chanterelles, silent as ghosts, constantly making sure they weren't being followed, so jealously they guarded their mushroom territory, and they didn't let the girls come with them, either. At the end of September, it was walnuts and chestnuts, and a few corncobs stolen from the fields just before harvest, which they cooked on the wood stove and drizzled with butter. They felt important: they were contributing to the life of the family by bringing food in now and again. But when they brought home a hen they'd pilfered from the far end of town, Olive gave them a hiding they weren't about to forget.

Eighteen months at Olive's place.
Eighteen months with Jojo, Anaïs and Manon.
Life was giving him bearings.
Life was giving him a breather.
And when, one morning in July, Corentin got up at the same time as the others, he didn't know—none of them knew—that this would be their last day together.

Marie showed up without warning.

Corentin's memories were scattered, but one stayed firmly in his mind: when Marie arrived unannounced, it was a bad sign.

She owed Olive money, naturally. She didn't give a damn. She had her big mouth, she could yell and weep. In any case, that day, that wasn't why she was coming.

Unlike the other times.

When she just showed up like that, it meant it was time to go. It meant she was taking her brat with her, dragging him by the arm. She shouted all the way from the house to the car, she left no void, not a snatch of silence, she took all the space. All so that she wouldn't have to apologize for having disappeared, so she wouldn't have to hear how worthless she was. So she wouldn't have to pay what she owed.

Over time, the friends, and babysitters—their frightened gazes trained on Corentin—over time those friends and nannies just let her go.

But in eighteen months, Corentin hadn't forgotten.

That was why on that particular morning, when the sound of the engine in the courtyard made them look up, and Olive turned her astonished gaze to him, he knew what she was going to say.

It's your mother, Corentin.

He burst into tears.

* * *

Marie came in and looked at them, the four little children with their round eyes staring at her. She gave an impatient jerk of her head and Olive sent the children outside. She told Corentin and Jojo to look after the little girls.

Anaïs didn't want to go out.

What are we going to do?

But she got up anyway, she knew she couldn't argue with Olive.

The four of them went by and Marie scolded her son, a sentence like a slap—There you go, crying as usual.

Outside, they couldn't be seen.

They sat on the little stone wall and Jojo murmured: You're going to go away.

Corentin began shouting: No, no!

I'll bet you anything you are, insisted Anaïs.

Manon's thin little voice—she was not yet three years old—asking again to make sure: Are you going away?

So Corentin went off on his own, the way a sickly animal will do, and he waited. He found a little stick and began drawing in the dirt. Lines. Circles. Anything. Then he abruptly started bashing the stick in the grass, searching through it with angry gestures, as if stabbing an old enemy. The earth was bleeding. So was he, from a sharp splinter that had torn open a flap of skin. He watched the red drops falling, leaving a colored rut on his finger. The ground soaked up the drops. You couldn't see them anymore.

And then Olive called the children back into the house. They ran to her, giving Marie and her mean expression a wide berth, they were ready to go and hide in their rooms, far from the tension they could sense even though they didn't understand it. Olive's tone stopped them in their tracks.

No.

She looked at Corentin.

You.

You're coming with me.

In the boys' room, she placed his belongings at the bottom of a canvas bag; they didn't take up much space. She could fit the ragdoll rabbit he slept with every night, so she put it in, too. And then a little brioche she'd baked the day before. Before they left the room, Olive ruffled Corentin's hair. She opened her mouth as if she were about to say something, but nothing came out. She kept silent. He was holding her hand— he thought he would never let go of that hand.

Marie was no longer in the other room. She had gone out and was leaning against the car door.

She couldn't help but see the tears on the little boy's cheeks, tears that wouldn't stop.

Get in, she said.

She tossed the bag with his belongings onto the back seat next to him. She started the ignition and Corentin turned around on the seat. Behind him, Olive and the children were waving goodbye, and he couldn't help it: he burst into tears.

Shut up, shouted Marie.

Oh, the silence.

Later, because she'd been hard on the kid, she murmured a few words. Said she was taking him to a magnificent place. That it was going to be wonderful.

She said that every time.

Corentin didn't listen. He was like one of those lambs that's been parted from its mother, bleating its heart out for days on end in the sheepfold where they've all been locked up, frightened and lost, bashing against the walls in a futile effort to knock them down, falling silent at last from exhaustion.

Corentin was crying because his mother had come back.

And yet for so long he'd dreamt of that moment. Dreams are nothing but lies.

* * *

The weather was fine that day, and it wasn't fair.

He was too unhappy.

Once again something unfamiliar was beginning, without joy, without eagerness. A tiny upset. A little boy in a red car weeping in silence: it wouldn't change anything in the world.

The trees had started shedding patches of bark.

* * *

Marie knew that life was shit.

She could tell—from the tedium of her waitressing work, from her pitiful salary, from the men who never stayed. She could tell from her shabby one-bedroom apartment, crushed among the attics in the Big City, where in winter she froze and in summer she roasted.

Nothing went her way.

She'd been angry for five years.

Angry with men, angry with other people who never helped, angry with the whole world.

But she wouldn't let them get away with it.

She hadn't given up yet. She had a future, she still believed in it. That was why she was driving toward the Forests.

Because she was angriest of all with the two grandmothers. She had never forgotten what they had done. The old women who'd stopped her from getting rid of the kid when he was no more than a drop of piss; the old women who'd set in motion something that might never have been.

She glanced over her shoulder at Corentin, asleep at last.

Corentin with his tangled black hair and his intense dark

gaze. The same eyes, the same way of holding himself, the same irresistible, unbearable charm. Corentin was Marc's son.

Worse luck: he was the wrong one, it would have been better if he'd been Jérémie's son, he'd been her husband back then, after all, it would have made things easier.

But for all that it would change . . .

And above all, why hadn't she thought of it sooner.

Old Augustine would remember her for sure, from this day forward.

She met her own gaze in the rear-view mirror and held back a smile.

At noon, Marie stopped to get gas and buy a bottle of water and two sandwiches. She said: Only two more hours.

Corentin didn't understand, or he wasn't listening. He was looking out the window. He hadn't said a word since they left. Stubborn brat, thought Marie.

The weather was still fine, very mild. She had the windows open. A fifty-fifty chance Marie'd end up with a sore throat, she didn't care, it was stifling in the car, with the kid's dark, silent gaze landing on her as he scanned the landscape from left to right.

Thirty miles to go: she cheered herself on in a muted voice, nearly there, nearly there.

It was two o'clock in the afternoon when she signaled for the turn-off to the village. Her heart was beating too fast. So long as they didn't run into anyone.

A minor road, and then a dirt track, to the right.

She turned in slowly. She stopped. She knew it was there, further back, fifty or eighty yards from there. Beyond the bend and the trees. She recognized it, the memories were coming back to her as if it were yesterday. If she went any closer, they'd see her from the house. So, she got out of the car. The little boy was looking at her.

She took his canvas bag and opened the door.

Come on.

He didn't move. She tugged him by the hand, and he slid out of the car.

She put his bag on his shoulder.

There.

She held one arm stretched out in front of her.

You see the path?

Just after it, just beyond the trees, there's a house. That's where you're going. There will be a lady there, an old lady. You give her this letter—she stuffed an envelope in his hand, which he dropped, at first.

Don't lose it.

Do you understand?

The little boy still didn't move, didn't shake his head, said nothing. So, Marie gave him a shove in his back.

That way.

She left him. Climbed back in the car.

He turned around to look at her. She gave a wave of her hand to tell him to go. Then rolled down the window.

Go on! Go!

He took one step.

Marie put the gear into reverse, but didn't move. Just ready to get out of there. Corentin had stopped and was looking at her again. She hated those big eyes full of tears, it gave her a twinge of some vague thing inside. Frowning, she wiggled her finger toward the path. So, he began walking slowly, tilting his head as if he was trying to see what was hidden behind the trees, hesitating, fearful. Marie wished she could nudge him along with the bumper to make him go faster.

There, he was out of sight.

No.

He was coming back.

This time, Marie got halfway out of the car, her anger getting the better of her.

Beat it, shit!

As if he were a dog, but she didn't know what else to say.

The little boy gave a start. He turned around.

Beyond the trees, he had seen the house and the lady. He was the only one who could see them, because Marie had stayed on the far side of the bend in the road.

An old house, and an old lady.

Who saw him, in turn, and slowly stood up straight from her garden where she'd been working. Of course, she wondered what was the meaning of this lost little boy.

Now he went closer, trembling.

He said nothing.

He handed her the envelope with her name clearly written on it, in detached capital letters: A U G U S T I N E.

* * *

The old woman's hard gaze on him. Not a smile, not a gesture.

She simply dropped the letter she had just read, and it stuck to the damp ground, which she had watered not fifteen minutes earlier. There were a few seconds of terrible silence. And then, walking on the crumpled paper, she took a step toward Corentin.

He ran away.

U-turn, then running flat out, he got past the bend going the opposite direction, calling for his mother in a shrill voice, come get me, don't leave me here.

The car had vanished. Even the smell of gas that often escaped from the old engine had evaporated; Marie must have accelerated like crazy, she was already far away.

The empty road. It would be the last memory.

He wouldn't forget any of it, not the long silent journey, nor the moment she had made him get out of the car, nor the letter she had made him take. He wouldn't forget the little path up to the bend, and his breathing getting faster, and the fear deep inside.

And finally, he would not forget the last words his mother said to him.

Beat it, shit!

* * *

A slate roof, damaged along the eaves, dreary stone with squat doorways, as if it didn't want to let anyone in. Augustine's house was ugly. Inside, from four o'clock on, you had to sit by the window if you wanted to read or do some mending. The tile floor was cracked in several places, speckled black-and-white tiles that you could stare at for hours trying to make out a pattern, and where you could barely see the dead insects.

Two ageless green armchairs, a coffee table cluttered with newspapers.

The old cat lying on the newspapers. That was the first thing Corentin saw.

In Augustine's house everything was cold, silent, old-fashioned. Corentin had never felt more alone. Alone with the old cat, with its stinky breath from its rotten teeth, but it was very gentle all the same.

Every night the little boy wept himself to sleep, stifling his tears in the sheets so that Augustine wouldn't hear him, he didn't want her to hear him, he didn't want her to console him.

Marie would come back for him. She couldn't leave him there, with this seventy-six-year-old woman who never laughed.

It would only be for a few days.

A few weeks.

Time went by with terrifying slowness.

Corentin would never see Marie again.

A little bit of summer still lingered in the Forests. Cautiously, Corentin explored the small village, it was really only a hamlet, a few houses scattered between the top and the bottom of the valley, a microcosm you could go around in no time. Augustine let him roam wherever he liked, she wasn't afraid he would get lost or that he would run away—where would he go?

He found it easier to situate the neighbors than the strange ties that bound him to this old woman (a great-grandmother, when you haven't known your own father, was meaningless; she explained it to him—I am your daddy's grandmother—but who was his father? And the father of his father? Augustine was too remote, too old for him to understand).

Too sudden, as well.

He was afraid of her. She looked like a bird of prey—severe, emaciated. At night, he would wake up, anxious, not daring to move. He waited for his eyes to adjust to the semi-darkness. He peered through the obscurity at the sleeping figure in the other bed and listened to the faint snoring punctuating his sleeplessness.

* * *

Initially, Augustine had put Corentin in the attic. To get there, you went up an outside stairway. It was the only place where she could give him a room; downstairs was all open space. She came to get him in the morning for breakfast, he mustn't move until she was ready. That was the rule.

She changed her mind after a week had gone by when she noticed that the boy was always awake when she opened the door upstairs: he was dressed, standing to attention, his eyes made wide by some emotion she could only assume was fear, and then she remembered that he was unfamiliar with the great dark woods, the sounds of the night, the deafening silence of ancient countryside.

He did not know the Forests.

A territory unto itself, colossal, thick with centuries-old trees, with pathways that disappeared through the seasons with the force of nature.

An evil territory, or so some said, they no longer knew why, but it was a reflex, whenever some misfortune befell someone in these parts, the old women and the old men wrung their hands and nodded their heads: it's the Forests.

Nothing good ever came up from this meager earth, everything died, it was too hot, or too damp, the soil was teeming with those insects that eat plants at the root, there was nothing but loose stones, the flanks of livestock were hollow, there was nothing to be done.

Nothing good, either, in the hearts of its people; their hearts had dried up generations ago.

And they all knew it: the heavens had abandoned them. The heavens had given up on them and turned to gentler regions. There was nothing more to be gained from this place, ever.

The people should have left long ago; none of them had.

They should have let the creepers and the trees destroy the little they had built in five hundred years—wretched houses, wretched crops, wretched memories. But they had no idea where to go; to be honest, they had no idea at all. That was why they had stayed. To wrench enough from the ground in order to survive from one day to the next took all their time, all their energy. They had no strength for the future, for dreams.

Only the dead left this land.

In that strange vastness, Corentin took up a tiny amount of space, stolen from who knew what presence, disrupting who knew what vibration in the sky. There was something disturbing about his intrusion; the atmosphere, particles of air, a fluttering in the world had to move ever so slightly to one side to let him in, bearings had to be shifted, places found all over again.

Augustine brought down the mattress that had been in the attic for years and laid it sideways to her own, feet to feet, in the corner where she slept.

* * *

There were no bedrooms downstairs: Augustine lived in a house that had only one—big—room, because she only had wood to heat it. In the overlarge hearth of the north gable end chimney, she had installed a wood-burning stove. In that way the heat—if you could call it that, the weak draft of tepid air that struggled to spread through the house in winter—would not be blocked by any walls.

At the outset, Augustine had not intended to share her territory with the boy; she learned to sleep with his restless presence, his nightmares, his fears. Did she know that he in turn was watching her as she snored during the night; that he studied her gaping mouth, the slight hook of her nose, the blanket that rose and fell to the rhythm of her breathing? There was no way of knowing, in any case she never mentioned it, and bit by bit, he came to find her more intriguing than terrifying in the moon-hatched shadow (Augustine never closed the shutters, and Corentin liked to see the pale glow of the orb casting gray through the room on cloudless nights).

Whenever he could, he escaped from the house buried deep in the valley. There was life elsewhere, there was laughter. There was something else besides work, besides Augustine's endless silences. He would run up the path, and the world was there.

At the top of the path to the right, five or six hundred yards from the house, there was Adèle, the neighbor Augustine didn't want him to go and see because she was dirty.

A bit further along was the Gentil farm where they raised cows. Once they had finished their chores, the children, Mathilde and Jeannot, played with Corentin; they had taken to each other very quickly. Corentin decreed that he and Mathilde would get married when they grew up. She laughed because she was two years older than him, so it wouldn't be possible, the bride is always younger.

Really?

Always.

In the next house over, at the entrance to the village, the house with the purple shutters, there lived an old man no one ever saw, and people said he'd been disfigured during the war, not by weapons, however, but by *experiments*.

Oh, said Corentin when Jeannot explained that the man's eyes were no longer level with each other.

He acted as if he knew. He dreamt of seeing him for real, but the mutilated man never left his house.

After the old man, there were the Dutch, then the retired couple with the pretty garden, then the English, then the Joris woman who was raising her four sons on her own.

Then came the old tart: Corentin didn't know her real name because everyone called her the old tart. She hid behind her curtain and took note of everything people were doing, and at what time, when they left, when they returned, whether they were alone or not, whether they had shopping bags, did they have their wood delivered, did they argue, did they have dinner with friends and if so, which ones.

And finally, there was Alice, and Corentin was under strict orders from Augustine not to speak to her. He made a detour so that she wouldn't see him go by. Augustine said she was crazy.

On the left-hand side of the road, there were only three houses. The first one belonged to Francis, a retired military man who didn't live there all year round, but he showed Corentin how to carve a piece of oak, how to repair a fence, how to set up a cage for rabbits. Francis hated his neighbor, Verdière, a nasty piece of work, he said, don't go anywhere near.

Corentin didn't.

You could hear the Verdière missus shouting clear to the end of the valley when she was calling her kids.

It made Francis laugh.

See what I mean.

Corentin imitated him, put his hands on his hips to listen.

Nasty piece of work, he said—and Francis laughed even louder.

The last house was abandoned. The ivy had brought down part of one wall, you could walk right in from around the back. The kids went to hide in there, to hunt for treasures, to make up a million stories.

* * *

And so Corentin got used to this life, too.

Used to the village, to the people, to school, which enthralled him.

And to Augustine—above all.

It took him a long time to realize that she loved him deeply. No one had ever loved him, Marie for a start. He'd gotten used to it. It must have been his own fault, he thought.

But then came old Augustine.

It was so strange. It was disturbing.

Oh, in her way. No cuddles or kisses. Just little signs of attention. Little moments spent together, tying up the beans or putting the wood away; when the hens got out, when the apples were ripe, when they had to bury the old cat who died because the years had gone by.

A sort of bitter gentleness, a kindly roughness.

A figure pretending to put away a spade or a rake when the bus dropped him off at the top of the road in the evening after school. No doubt counting the five or six minutes it would take him to come down the path, sometimes ten, when he would stop to pick a daisy or a honeysuckle vine to give to her when he got home.

Augustine secretly watching out for him, with a smile of pretend surprise once he appeared in the little bend before the house. She would take the small bouquet in her hand and they would go get a vase.

Together, they watered the vegetable garden, weeded the courtyard, tidied the flower beds. They ate what Augustine had prepared during the day, fresh vegetables, or ones from the freezer where she carefully laid in every crop; noodles, pies, terrines that she would exchange with neighbors for some fruit from their orchard, or sometimes a helping of meat, when on a Thursday she'd gone to wait for the butcher's round and come back with her meager treasure, double-checking the coins she'd been handed as change.

They planted some nasturtiums where they'd buried the cat.

When Augustine was angry—when the bills arrived, when the rabbits nibbled the lettuce at night, when in the evening on television they showed nothing but rubbish and she had no strength left for anything but distraction—Corentin would place his little hand on her wrinkled one, and with his black eyes, look deep into her old, faded gaze. It took a minute or two, or even longer, and then Augustine began to smile again. Life started up. Time moved forward again.

*

Marie didn't come back. Whenever a car strayed to the top of their path, Corentin was surprised to find himself praying it wasn't her. She was like a shadow slowly retreating, but a gust of wind might bring her back at any moment.

Augustine was protecting him, he thought.

She didn't ask for money to have him stay there. This was something of a wonder to him. There was nothing but her.

She didn't scold him.

He wasn't scoldable. He'd made her little habits and needs his own, he took her as his guide. To go to the garden, to fetch dead branches for kindling, he followed in her footsteps. He imitated her gestures. Even the tone of her voice: he tried to make his own sound hoarse. Only once did he oppose her, when he found a kitten on the path and brought it home. She didn't want it. Corentin let it sleep in his bed, and they discussed the matter no further.

When it came to important things—that was how she put it, important things—she wouldn't give in to him. Not when it came to the garden, or the village, or school above all.

Always decent and always first. There is no other way.

That was how he began to grow up.

C orentin turned ten.

The oldest trees had begun to dry out, the summers were too severe. Most of the streams where he used to wade, before, had become trickles of water smelling of silt. Every week on television he heard the words climate change, two degrees, three degrees, danger. It meant nothing to him. It was hot, that was all. Hot and dry. The old people around here talked about 1976, they'd seen it before. It was nature, that's all. Naturally some things had changed: the previous summer, there had been praying mantises in people's gardens. They'd never seen any before; ordinarily the insects live some two hundred and fifty miles farther south. Now they'd moved higher up, it was a sign. But things had always changed; that was life, too.

Augustine was slowly getting old. Like the trees. With the same wrinkled skin, gnarled, a little more twisted than before because of arthritis.

Every evening they looked at the sky together. When it was clear, she taught him the stars. When there was cloud or rain, she told him stories. Sweltering in the heat or bundled in their coats, they would look up at the sky, and the light went deep into their eyes. Augustine had stopped helping Corentin with his homework; she couldn't get a grasp of it anymore. But the evenings were for him. She reigned over the world, over infinity, over the thousands of stories and legends hidden deep in the Forests.

They went to sleep in separate rooms now: timidly, Corentin had asked to move back into the attic. He wasn't afraid anymore. He'd grown big—too big. He didn't want Augustine to see him getting undressed at night, and it would be tricky to slip behind a length of wall or an open door when there were so few of them.

The attic became his world. In winter he slept in the little walled room at the back, against the chimney, which lent some enveloping warmth. In summer, he stayed in the attic's large open space, his eyes riveted on the stars dancing beyond the open shutters; when there was wind, the branches of the fir tree came to scratch against the window, it was a sort of music, he fell asleep feeling nothing bad could happen.

* * *

On his way home from school, Corentin often stopped off at Adèle's. Her place smelled stuffy, of wood, of Adèle. He inhaled deeply, his nose filled with the scent of her eau de Cologne, rose perfume, and powder. She wears perfume because she doesn't wash, grumbled Augustine. Corentin didn't care. Adèle's place smelled good.

It was a refuge for Corentin—and for so many others, because the house was always open. A dog, a few cats, Jeannot and Mathilde often came over, and one or two other kids, birds on the windowsills. There were bones, and saucers of milk, and candies, and bits of bacon.

Adèle was a seamstress, the sort of items and garments that were so fine that people came all the way from town for them.

At the same time, Adèle passed on the odd flea or louse.

You see, shouted Augustine, reaching for her bottle of citronella or lavender.

Corentin kept going there all the same.

When she turned fifteen, Mathilde declared that she wouldn't marry Corentin.

She'd made a decision no one had seen coming: to become a nun. What had she been reading, what had she heard, what did she imagine? She had the exalted air and large crazed eyes of adolescent girls who find God. She was absolutely certain that one day He would appear before her—God or Mary, she almost hoped it would be Mary, she felt so close to her. Like Bernadette Soubirous, Lúcia dos Santos, and Maria Esperanza, there would be Mathilde.

Corentin tried to reason with her. These were schoolgirls' stories, all a joke, he asserted. And besides, it didn't just happen because you decided it would. But she didn't listen. She didn't hear. She really believed in it all, there was nothing to be said, nothing to be done, and she pushed him away, more and more sharply. He understood that she had begun to look down on him; he was only a boy, but she, Mathilde, was waiting for the Holy Virgin. She spoke of it as if it were about to happen. She would say, *my apparition.* Corentin despised her, and the Virgin Mary, and life and everything else. He despised this faith he was powerless against—in revenge, he called Mathilde *that fat cow.*

He sobbed in his bed that night; that was the end of love.

They stopped speaking. Before long she stopped going to school, she had work on the farm. They no longer ran into each other. So Corentin vented his anger to Jeannot.

That fat cow, he said over and over.

Jeannot nodded.

* * *

There were the promises.

Before she died, Augustine wanted to see the sea.

You're not going to die, said Corentin, looking at her old hands, which had begun to tremble.

She smiled. With him she always smiled, now that he was almost grown up; he was a full head taller than she was, but it's true she wasn't very tall.

One day it all has to come to an end, she murmured, looking out the window.

But not right away.

No. Not right away.

I'll take you to see the sea, before that.

All right.

Too easy, promises.

* * *

And because the school had noticed him, when he was eighteen Corentin left for the Big City.

Augustine brushed it away with a wave of her hand: his hesitations, doubt, fears, his guilt at leaving her by herself. The words that stayed on her lips, stretched wide in a smile: you're going to be a professor.

He left.

She didn't go to see him off at the station, you had to walk, wait for the bus, walk some more. She was keeping her strength for when he came back.

Of course I'll come back, he promised.

Of course you will.

And he came back, like he said. Both the same and so different: with the mark of the Big City, which fascinated and absorbed him.

He told Augustine all about it. He was discovering everything—the long streets, the dense crowds, the never-ending noise. He had friends, they were remaking the world. His voice, the gleam in his eyes, brought it all home to Augustine: science and literature, lights, music, nights that were never over because you mustn't waste an instant of such a life. Yes, there was all that in his eyes, with their flame of joy, you could read it there, see it there.

He was enchanted.

Do you understand? he asked. Can you picture what it's like?

She tried to make it a yes. Was it so very different from what she saw on television, and which frightened her a bit—all that Corentin gave off of the buzz, the fusion of thousands of inexhaustible lives, light, high-spirited, urgent, everything moving quickly and loudly, everything skimming past without ever stopping, everything falling silent yet the noise continuing, the days went by and it never got dark, it was nothing but glow, radiance, conflagration.

Sitting by her television, Augustine worried. And Corentin, shouting with excitement and love, breathed in the city, savored it. Augustine could not tell him that it wouldn't last, she didn't dare say the words that came to her and spoke of falsehood. Corentin was happy, that was enough.

In the Forests, the leaves were already falling from the trees. It was June, Corentin was finishing his first year of studies. The seasons were getting ahead of themselves, out of sync, confused. They had changed—everything was changing, imperceptibly.

* * *

During the autumn, Corentin didn't come back as often. His head was still spinning with so many new, brilliant things, he felt as if he would never manage to see everything or do everything, an entire life would not suffice, he was consumed. A little butterfly full of wonder, dazzled, open-winged.

Augustine waited a little longer. There was no bitterness. She knew that soon enough he would let her know he was on his way, she was patient, even if time counted double for her, at her age, everything could come to an abrupt end. She watched television thinking that Corentin was in there some- where, in that strange world he'd taken to so well.

He was there and one day he would be here with his joyful, dazzling, whirling presence.

He wrote to ask forgiveness for his absence.

On the phone, Augustine had trouble hearing him.

You know, about the sea. I haven't forgotten.

She said: We'll see.

Soon he came for Christmas and then a few days in summer. He thought about Augustine often, in the Big City. And then he told her about those moments, early mornings when he felt restless, long nights full of wonder at the lights reflected in the river. Sometimes he was unhappy to see so little of her. Augustine shook her head, she wouldn't allow it. When he was there, she accepted these moments of celebration without a sigh, unconditionally. She didn't wonder when he would be back. There was no pleading in the depths of her gaze.

Everything was normal.

And so it goes with children: they go away.

Corentin didn't know what friends were. In the Forests, there were some children, of course, who'd become adolescents, then very young adults. After school they had always gone their separate ways, each of them to their own house. Social life stopped at five o'clock, scattering children into old, isolated buildings. After that came family. After that came more work, livestock, crops, the household, the multitude of little chores that left no free time, free time was television, and social networks at night, when they should have been sleeping and they rediscovered one another from an unexpected angle, and they recognized each other, spoke at last—then the following morning everything was back in its place, everything was set, rigid again.

But the Big City brought so many people with it.

In the beginning, Corentin's way was to keep quiet, on the sidelines, trying to laugh along with the others, without much conviction, because the others laughed all the time, and he had figured out he would have to be like them. In the beginning he had watched them—he had imitated them. He didn't know how to laugh the way they did, it was too loud, too noisy, it was something that wasn't just joyful but also a bit crazy, uncontrollable, excessive—that was the word that came to him. Sometimes he felt as if his jaw had gotten stuck, pulled backwards. But it was enough to belong. He opened his mouth. He screwed up his eyes. It was close enough—he laughed as best he could, it didn't matter that he was pretending, it worked.

Bit by bit, he stopped accepting everything that came his way and he chose his friends. It took some time. People who spoke, made things up, sang, shouted too, and yet. He liked them, he thought, as he stole glances at them. This was his life now, his world. There was no more solitude. They'd all adopted each other. It was very different from before. It was a fine thing.

From his window he observed the night-time city just there, within reach.

* * *

They were twelve in number.

Twelve students who had grown up, who were about to become professors, thrown together in university auditoriums or cafeterias, biologists, geneticists, geologists now, and there was Luna, who had specialized in those strange water sciences she whispered into his ear at night when they weren't sleeping.

Twelve of them: a group, a clan, a tribe. They had that strength. For three years, then five, then eight, they'd been together—competing, complementing, enriching one another with thoughts they hadn't even known they had, gradually becoming conscious of the ties they must forge, because the world was not an enclosed place, it was people who had compartmentalized it, you could only understand things if you had a global vision. Together the twelve of them had the world at their fingertips.

They often met up in the evening, as if returning to the promise of a magical interlude, feverishly, their thoughts already pounding in their brains, and every time they knew: for the space of an hour, or a few days, they would remake the world.

They searched for a hideout, a cocoon, somewhere they'd be sheltered from everything, where no one would come to disturb their endless discussions, where nothing and no one could stop the flow of their too-eager ideas, or the fusion among them, or the fug of alcohol to forget that life was not as gorgeous as they had told it to be, not as thrilling as they had hoped, but they had to live that life, because it was all they had—that, and the twelve of them both distant and so close, friends, rivals, enemies, absolutely vital in the end.

* * *

Corentin felt too hot, parched. The city slaked his thirst.

The city, silted up. The city sticky, thick, opaque. There was not enough air. Everything arrived muffled and screaming at the same time. The noise clashed with the silence of great fear.

And yet everything carried on as usual.

You couldn't see that it would take only a tiny little thing for it all to burst into flames. For it all to collapse.

It was already in his throat, perhaps, in that tiny burning sensation when he swallowed, in his sour saliva.

Go on. It was so much more than that.

But in the city, you couldn't see that nature was dying. It had no effect on the asphalt or the streetlamps. It did not change the students' singing, or the sound of car horns. It did not lessen the laughter or shouting, or doors creaking open and shut, or the rumble of the subway, or the ring tones of cell phones.

It did not change the color of the sky—because no one was looking. There was too much light there before them. Artificial light.

Turn it off, pleaded Corentin sometimes, in silence.

The world like a light bulb.

The world like a party, and it was almost midnight.

* * *

Eyes closed, sweat on his brow, his hand wiping it all night long.

Were there only the nights left?

The days went by, relentlessly.

Study, write, speak, listen, walk, drink, sleep.

Everything hanging on.

Everything hanging by a thread.

Is this what it meant, to be happy?

You would have had to record every moment of every day, in order to remember.

The twelve of them would get away together.

Every weekend, with the people he loved, Corentin went down into the bowels of the Big City. The air was even thinner. But at last, in the underground tunnels, they were cut off from the feverish agitation, the buzzing of the surface, the humming crowds.

Thirty, sixty feet below the street; they weren't interested in the ossuaries. Just the quiet. The peace.

They went beyond the places that were authorized, they knocked down walls and slipped through the breaches, never sure whether they would lead anywhere.

There was no more electricity. They took candles with them, like before.

They brought what they needed to drink. A lot. Too much. Deliberately.

They stayed until the lack of oxygen gave them headaches. They went back out at night, that same night or the following one, wandering through a different obscurity, through other dark shadows, so that the floating sensation would last. The sun always rose. They knew that every journey was only an illusion.

F ar from there, the Forests.

The thought came and Corentin brushed it away as if it were an insect, with a wave of his hand, a jerk of his head, a tired click of his tongue.

He had to go there—he should have gone there.

The desire gradually waned. Or rather, the desire was there, but nothing came of it.

Luna leaned over to kiss him, and, with a beer in his hand, he forgot again.

Except for the twinge deep in his gut.

Yes, he would go.

But not right now. Maybe tomorrow. Or later. After the partying, after the girls, after the exams at the end of the year—which would be the last ones.

If nothing came along in between time.

He felt guilty.

And then the feeling left him.

* * *

In the Forests, there was still air.

The harvests were over, and at last the sky was dusted free of those yellow particles that had blocked it for ten days. As the particles fell, they left a film on the streams that lingered stubbornly, deep in the little valleys, where wisps of cool air hid among the grasses, under stones.

Corentin didn't give a damn about the air.

Let there be drink.

Let there be love.

Let there be dreams.

The rest could go hang: nothing else mattered. Underground, that is what they had sworn

—beer, love, dreams.

They'd become a clan and they'd gone mad, their desire to live was too intense, as if everything were going to end. As if they might die tomorrow.

And they might.

Underneath the endless partying, a strange fear was eating at their guts, dulling their laughter, opening their eyes wider.

Maybe it was life that was scaring them—that moment when they would have to seize hold of it, since their years of study were coming to an end, and they could tell that an era was slowly ending, and not just an era—a way of life, a world. They didn't really want it that badly, the life of the fully adult individual, where everything becomes irreversible, everything becomes serious. They would be going their separate ways, because there would be work, and money, and glory, they would leave, scatter, and miss each other forever.

Was that what was holding them back?

It was late spring and it was hard to breathe, and none of them cared, but through their open mouths as they tried to inhale a little more, they could tell: there was something not right.

Maybe it came from their imminent separation, to start the ordinary life that lay in ambush, and everything they were going to lose, and they were so acutely conscious of the fact, although they couldn't say it, couldn't admit it to themselves, because it hurt too much, and they were already protecting themselves.

There was that, and more, too, something that wasn't right

inside, and something that wasn't right outside—in the world. But they'd already said that, the year before, and for those who were already there, even the years before that, so it was nothing new.

Nothing was going as it should, and never did.

Well then. Because everything was in balance.

They became tightrope walkers. Beneath their feet was an abyss. They didn't look down. They didn't dare. They spread their arms to keep from slipping. The bowels of the earth beckoned to them, as if to some indestructible cocoon.

And they went on partying.

Like forced laughter that makes no one laugh, and which prints grimaces on exhausted faces.

You look like crap, Corentin.

They all looked like crap.

They stared at each other in their hole far beneath the asphalt, they noticed their pallid features, the dark circles under their eyes, the pinched nostrils of the ones who were breathing in short gasps, and yet they were breathing, and they splattered each other with gold, sequins of alcohol that floated into their mouths and down their throats, dampening their skin, stinging.

Back there, Augustine had been sleeping for a long time.

While they were still singing, she was getting up to make coffee.

They were sweating with beer and heat.

She opened the windows, shook out the pillow, listened to the nightingale that didn't know anymore whether it was day or night. The sun didn't show its face. The heat was gray, the humidity made one's fingers sticky. Augustine closed the windows, closed the useless shutters, washed the old cracked tile floor. She went down into the cellar where the temperature stayed more pleasant.

As for them, they slept all together in a restless tangle, drops of sweat on their bodies and brows, which gave a sheen to their faces, to their hair, disheveled or pulled back. As for them, they didn't want to wake, they didn't want to go back above ground, they pretended to sleep, nodded off again, drifted in and out of sleep. They had visions. They didn't remember them.

Luna sometimes snuggled close to someone else. Corentin didn't say anything. That didn't matter either. Like the others, he was no longer sure of what really mattered, what was worth standing up and fighting for, he didn't know anymore, he let himself go with the tide.

They passed their bottles along in a semi-conscious stupor. The sound of clinking glass made their heads throb.

What more might they have heard?

A long sentence was uttered in the middle of the night, tapping against the walls, fading away in silence.

What are we going to do.

It was not a question.

What are we going to do.

After.

But after what, no one said. The time at university was coming to an end, that must have been it, they were all thinking about that.

After our studies, ventured a drawling voice.

No, not that. After everything.

After everything.

They laughed, quietly.

And that tiny laugh, that tiny sound, is that what held them back? They didn't hear it coming.

But there could be no doubt.

And if they had a moment's doubt, a little later, it would vanish all of a sudden. Once they decided to go back above ground—for those of them who would go back. Once they opened the door, when they'd slide the bent iron manhole cover along the still-warm pavement.

And that, yes, that would be after.

Because for now, this was the end of the world.

It was the end of the world and they knew nothing about it.

Buried underground, buried in alcohol and dreams. They had drunk so much, taken in so much, struggled so hard for the thoughts they had to convey and defend. They had gone down under the asphalt and the cars, their arms laden with supplies, their headaches already pounding against their temples and they were looking forward to it already. To losing their bearings, going deep, letting themselves go under. They would come back full of hallucinations, full of poetry.

Full of melancholy.

Or they would not come back.

They said it with a laugh, every time, when the moment came to slip underground and feel the darkness seize them bodily.

They said it to be provocative—or because of one of those superstitious notions they held in contempt, but which were rooted deep in their souls.

Their partying—they murmured the word, trembling with joy.

Their partying saved them at the same time as it distanced them from the world, but they didn't want the world, not for an instant did they imagine that it might be the world that didn't want them anymore.

They were protected by the earth.

Buried underground like animals.

And it wasn't true that they knew nothing about it.

But they would never learn the truth about what happened.

And it wasn't true that they didn't hear anything.

There was that strange noise in the background, a clamor that came to them, somehow muffled. But they thought it was in their minds. It was in their fogginess.

And then there was the rumbling sound.

So when they saw the ceiling shaking, they stood up. The darkness was swaying.

Then they felt it.

The earthquake.

Or so they thought, because it wasn't an earthquake. Or not only. It was something much bigger: something total.

Since they didn't know what was going on, they looked at each other and panicked. It began with one of the boys setting off into the tunnel, running toward the way out. And it was like an alarm, like the signal they had all been waiting for, to unfold their stiff, clumsy bodies. They took off after him.

A few of them.

The ones who were not too groggy, not too drunk—not too far gone into the depths of their own souls, where a force held them, stopped them from going back up. Those ones got the hell out of there as best they could, uncertain, their hands feeling for the limestone walls to keep from falling.

The other ones—they couldn't get up. Couldn't run. They watched their friends staggering, fleeing, and they could still feel the earth vibrating beneath their bellies, but they stayed there, glued to the ground by some dizziness that made them suddenly throw up, they heard the scrambling and shouts, and they were frightened.

But their bodies refused to move. Their will had become worthless. They had tears in their eyes, they wanted to call out for help. They kept silent. They were alone. Corentin was among them.

He too had his eyes open wide, his lips frozen around a scream that did not come. He too knew it was time to go—and he couldn't. He had watched the others stepping over his legs, he had tried to grab hold of one of them to lift himself up, to find a shoulder to lean on, to leave the low-ceilinged room where the stones were coming loose one after the other. He remembered feeling pain, perhaps someone had kicked him to get past. Already, humanity was deserting.

Dying was much less fun than they'd thought.

They didn't want to die anymore.

But no one was asking them for their opinion.

To die brazenly was one thing—but to suffocate underground, beneath the rubble?

The ones who had stayed behind got to their knees. The candles were still burning, the bottles were set in a row, the food put away in boxes. They weren't thinking about that anymore. They were hardly thinking about getting away, they couldn't think straight; only fear could make its way into their guts.

It will pass, thought Corentin, closing his eyes.

He no longer saw their hesitant shadows in the tiny, dancing flames of the candles. He no longer saw their terrified, helpless gazes.

He didn't see, at the end of the tunnel, the seven friends who'd run away and who were grabbing at the metal ladder to climb back above ground. It changed nothing.

Nor did he hear their screams as they lifted the metal cover and pulled themselves outside, shoving one another in their haste.

Nor the scarcely human chirring that came from their throats the moment they thought they were safe, and those who had already climbed out collapsed to the ground, struck by some unknown blast, dead before they even reached the earth. The others fell back inside, tumbling down the ladder.

The metal cover fell back over them.

* * *

Luna had been the last among them.

That was what had saved her.

The six bodies who'd gone ahead of her, who were already outside or still inside, absorbed the fire, the radiation, the horror; she didn't know what was out there, didn't try to find out. Suffocating beneath the corpses, she struggled, shouting, shoving at arms and legs and torsos, wriggling as much as was humanly possible to get free. She didn't want to look at them. She'd had time enough to see. They were no longer men and women; they were like melted flesh, black stinking hides that grasped at her and pinned her to the ground, and it took her several minutes to pull herself out from under, to escape the weight of bodies, to curl up at last against the wall opposite her, trembling and sobbing, gasping for breath.

She stayed there—for how long, twenty, thirty seconds.

No time at all.

But it was huge.

Then she understood that some infinite shock wave had broken over the earth, setting fire to everything in its wake. She didn't know what it was, she didn't know where it had come from. But she'd heard it rumbling above her head, she could feel the heat that was trying to get into the tunnel, and she stood up on her trembling legs, backed her way to the end of the tunnel and, spinning around, joined the five others who had stayed in the little room, the five friends they'd abandoned without a thought, and she collapsed next to them.

She collapsed and found she could no longer speak.

The words jostled inside her, her body was betraying her now, she was paralyzed, seized up.

Later, she would think it didn't really matter—the others couldn't have understood what she had to say. She would have to wait a few hours for them to recover a semblance of consciousness, so that she could explain the inexplicable, so that the same fear that had been in the eyes of those who died would now be in all their eyes, all five of them—so that, instinctively, they would stagger to their feet, and she would put her hands on their arms and whisper: we mustn't go out.

* * *

So they waited.

And the longer they waited, not knowing what was happening above ground, the greater their terror.

They tried to ask Luna.

What happened?

What's wrong?

She shook her head—we mustn't go out.

They sat in a circle in their space with its dank air; they huddled together, with the candles and bottles. No one was thirsty anymore. No one felt like dreaming or loving. They shivered as if they had a high fever.

What happened?

What's going on?

Up there.

They wept.

What should we do?

We wait, said Luna.

They waited.

Never before had they listened so attentively, never before had they kept such cautious silence. They could hear themselves swallow. Their tense bodies were unraveling, their teeth were chattering in the stifling darkness.

It lasted for hours.

Then they were exhausted.

One by one, all six of them fell asleep.

* * *

They awoke and they couldn't say what time it was, or what day. Their watches and phones had stopped. The candles had burned to the end of the wick, it was pitch black. As if they were blind.

They opened their eyes wide, like madmen. Maybe they thought it would let in some light—it did no such thing.

What shall we do?

They listened to the silence.

It's stopped.

What's stopped?

The thing.

But no one dared go out. It was too soon. The image of melted bodies that Luna had shared with them: they were haunted by that image, they were afraid, they had what they needed to last a few more days underground.

They stayed.

How long?

They rationed out the beer and the food. They refrained from eating, to make it last longer.

What day is it.

No one knew. They didn't expect an answer to the question—it was just to have something to say, to talk, to keep their voices from going any hoarser. To make sure, perhaps, that the others were still there, because the candles had gone out a long time ago.

They couldn't see each other. But they huddled together, again, shoulder to shoulder, holding hands. They reassured one another. Held each other. Still loved each other—a little.

They would die from all this waiting. It must have been seven or eight days, maybe more, surely no less.

From time to time, one of them would murmur.

We should go out now.

In the darkness, they nodded. But no one got up. No one wanted to go first—not one of them would admit as much.

They were hungry and it didn't matter. When they grew thirsty, that was another matter. They knew the moment was drawing near.

Shit, one of them said, when at last they decided to go above ground. Shit.

At the foot of the ladder, they looked at each other. They looked up. They tried not to see or smell the bodies of the others who had fallen, they avoided them with their feet, feeling their way carefully with their toes, don't touch, don't think.

Who's going first.

Their hearts were beating too fast. Suddenly they were not so thirsty, terror was dissolving them. They licked the sweat from their lips. Corentin stood there, eyes lowered. He was no better than the others, and his hands were trembling just like theirs. They had no idea what they would find up there. More than once, they said they'd got it wrong, that they would go up and everything would be like before. That they'd made it all up, imagined it, hallucinated. That years later they would all have a good laugh about it together. And remember it as if it were some strange experience.

But now, at the foot of the ladder, that seemed impossible.

There were the bodies at their feet, and their obvious terror.

And then up there—not a sound, as if the never-ending flow of traffic had vanished.

Of course something had happened. They were not sure they wanted to find out what. But they couldn't stay underground and, deep down, they really did want to find out.

It was just that they didn't want to die.

Albane was first to reach for the rungs of the ladder.

Corentin watched her with large frightened eyes. Albane was the best of them all. The most gifted, the most intuitive, the most methodical, too. She had a great career ahead of her: oddly, this was what he was thinking when he held up his hand.

Wait.

She shook her head.

We have to go now, don't we?

They watched as she climbed. Slowly. They could sense the sweat on her brow, down her face, falling at their feet as if it were raining.

Her head had reached the metal manhole cover, and she touched it with her fingertips and looked down at them.

Right.

She smiled.

A thrust of her lower body, a shove of her arm: she was out.

She didn't fall.

She didn't burn.

They saw her turn and sit immediately on the edge of the hole; her legs would not bear her weight anymore. From where they were, they could tell that she was trembling. She was making halting little sounds—sobs, panic, relief, they imagined everything. She sat there, not moving.

Are you okay?

She didn't answer. After a long moment she turned her head and looked down at them below.

And then they knew they could come up now too, and that they would regret it all their lives.

D evastation.

Was there another word for it?

Corentin was sitting next to Albane, among the others. Like them, he was looking all around.

But looking at what?

Every living thing had turned to ash.

Everything that had once existed had been destroyed.

All that remained were black, atrophied, burned contours: buildings, trees, cars.

People.

Everything so entirely destroyed that they could not understand, could not grasp what had happened. It was too much. Too empty. There was not even a sound, not a motor, nor a bird. Not even a voice. The asphalt had melted, the streets had become molten, then congealed in irregular waves, probably when everything had begun to cool off. The air was still too warm, heat rose from the ground, fell from the sky.

And they were there on the edge of this world they did not recognize. They stood there, shocked, stunned. They had no words. They looked at each other; stringing a sentence together was impossible. They turned their heads from left to right, they struggled to breathe. They wiped the sweat from their brows, and trembled.

After a long while, they saw two figures walking through the streets, gaunt creatures like themselves, arms dangling, hands empty.

Living people.

So there were some, still.

They stood up. They called out to them—but they didn't come. They shouted questions, tried to follow them.

What happened?

What caused it?

Does anyone know?

Where is everyone, where have the people gone?

But those they were calling to took to their heels and vanished. And they were so surprised that they froze, looking all around to see if there might be a reason why the others had fled, but there was nothing.

But a spark had been lit inside them. Something had stirred, surpassing astonishment and pain.

There were still people.

Suddenly, they all began shouting at the same time. Because their consciousness had returned, they were filled with alarm for the people they loved, they shouted that they were coming to find them. They clambered over the rubble, they didn't know which way to go, all their bearings had disappeared. But they kept going.

Fathers, mothers, brothers, sisters. Were they still alive? Some reflex rooted in their fingers made them take out their cell phones, they dialed numbers, started over because they could hear no dial tone and they weren't used to that; before, they could reach everybody, all the time. Then panic muddled their thoughts, they began to shout names into the great void. They shattered the silence. Their voices resounded against the still-steaming walls of buildings. There was no reply.

Corentin gazed at them in silence. It was astonishing to see these superior beings—wasn't that how they had seen themselves for years—resorting to the impulses of lowly beasts, their cries a croaking sound, scarcely human, a wailing, stifled rage, already certain of its pointlessness. It was both fascinating and chilling to hear their desperate appeal, the kind only children make when they believe they have been abandoned, those cries they make only when they are sure they are alone, so clearly do they signal a terrifying fragility. Corentin listened, trying to suppress the shivering of his skin, the tightness in his throat.

Suddenly that feeling came to him again, the hurt of not belonging. And indeed, he did not belong, he might have thought he did, but it wasn't true, since all their howling meant the same thing: the people they loved were somewhere else.

What illusion had brought them together for a time, as long as the world was in place, above all what falsehood on their part, for months and years, a sort of unchanging family that dissolved like a puff of smoke, a circus act, now you see them, now you don't. Deep down, what did they mean to one another?

They were mere silhouettes, scattering.

Nothing at all.

They all went their separate ways.

And he, Corentin, had no one to look for in the Big City, no one waiting for him.

He was the last one to leave. He stood for a long time in the spot where a short while earlier they had been sitting together, holding to each other like victims of a shipwreck clinging to pieces of driftwood. Maybe he hoped that one of them would come back for him, take him by the arm and lead him away.

Don't stay here.

They didn't come back. Corentin stopped waiting for them. It was just that it was too far away, where he had to go. Too far for him to go now, when dusk was falling, he didn't have the strength. The others had taken all his strength from him.

Tears flowed down his cheeks. Tears of anger, sorrow. He didn't love them either. But it hurt all the same. The hurt of solitude.

* * *

A strange night began to fall. The sky was gray and full of ash. Corentin walked through the Big City, his steps so small, so aimless, that he was probably going around in circles, but he couldn't be sure, all the streets looked the same, all the buildings were burned to cinders, the houses blasted, the roads cratered.

And even if it all looked the same, he couldn't stop himself from gazing all around. A sort of morbid fascination, he thought, one burned building after another, blackened walls, cars and motorcycles all the same melted gray and, above all, if he looked down, bodies immobilized everywhere, captured in the street, at the door to a shop, at the entrance to the metro.

In one store, its doors smashed open, Corentin took a blanket and a backpack. He sat down on the shattered tile floor, and then all at once he stretched out. He had no more strength. It was the shock, he thought, he was nothing but a long trembling envelope of empty flesh. He could go no farther. His legs wouldn't carry him.

How many of them were there still, on earth?

Not for one moment did the thought that rescuers might appear cross his mind. He knew that everything was lost. It had all burned. There was nothing left.

Hours later he fell asleep, after more wandering, shaken by silent sobs, damp with the tears he tried to crush in the blanket. Strange thoughts came to him: that if he stayed outside, he'd be devoured by mosquitoes. But all the insects had died, too, and nothing bit him.

He finally fell asleep because he had found his answer at last.

He also had someone to love.

It came all by itself, so obvious, so immense.

But it would take all his strength to get there. He had to sleep. It would take him days.

To find out whether Augustine was still alive.

It was morning and the city stank of death. Corentin had been awake for a long time. But his body—spread on the ground as if nailed.

Why should he get up, what for, huh?

And now, loudmouth that he'd been, telling anyone who'd listen how much he liked solitude, how he needed it, desired it. But that was before. Before he was really alone. It was very different from the way he used to envisage it.

He got to his knees at last. He howled.

Is there anyone out there!

He just couldn't do it, all alone. The journey to Augustine's terrified him, he would have to go through fire and void, it would take courage, and he didn't have courage.

Corentin rolled up into a ball like a sick cat. He pulled the blanket over him, over his face, so he wouldn't see what was around him.

Here, this was the world.

Everything had disappeared from the world from before. The earth had become too big. The sun was masked by layers of dust, but, in any case, Corentin didn't want to see the sun anymore. Under his blanket it was all gray. The sun would never rise again. So much the better. He was too hot, but the vastness outside terrified him. And so, he sweated under his blanket, sporadically gasping for air. His heartbeat slowed. He prayed this might be the end, when in fact he was just dozing off.

He gathered his strength—just enough to get up and go to see Augustine. This weakness made him want to weep, this fucking lethargy that glued him to the cracked pavement, but there was nothing left in his body, no more blood, no more warmth, he had to go looking for them deep in his guts, deep in his fear, drawing them up the way you draw a drop of water from a dry well, an exhausting task, an impossible effort.

And then the thought hit him like a slap in the face.

The others—the moment they climbed over the edge of the hole and saw the destruction of the world—the others had rushed off to find the people they loved.

And he just lay there, moaning. He'd been whining and sobbing since the day before—a pathetic coward.

Augustine.

He wrenched himself from the ground.

He felt dizzy, spread his arms not to fall.

Augustine—he set off in a random direction, straight ahead.

* * *

He was afraid he wouldn't find any food, afraid he wouldn't find any supplies. But stores were open and there was no one wandering around inside. No one watching. No one even stealing. There wouldn't be enough of them to take everything: entire aisles full of goods shaken by the thing—in his mind, Corentin would go on calling it *the thing*, because he didn't know what had happened—all these goods, waiting to be taken.

There, said Corentin over and over, it's not that no one wanted this stuff, but there was no one left.

He filled his bag as full as he could. As heavy as he was. It took him hours but it was a relief to be busy, a relief not to let his spirit go to the dogs, he had a goal, he focused on it.

Get away.

It was far, maybe two or three hundred miles.

Before, there were trains to get there.

But there were no more trains.

Or there were cars.

But there were none of those either.

Corentin looked at his legs, his feet, his shoes: that was what would get him there.

To Augustine.

He didn't know if she had survived.

Before, you would use the phone to find out.

But there was no more phone.

* * *

He worked out that it would take him fifteen days to get there.

From here, of course, he couldn't see them. But he knew: The Forests were fifteen days walking with a backpack that weighed as much as he did. He had found some sturdy hiking boots. The next thing was to stay strong.

What are fifteen days in a man's life?

But fifteen days to find what?

To hope what—that this thing had stopped at the entrance to the Forests, that they had made it through, that there were survivors.

He mustn't think about it. If he thought about it, he would sit down in the street and never move again, because nothing seemed possible. He would sit down and wait. He mustn't either think or sit down.

Just go.

Put one foot after the other without thinking, because thinking meant stopping. What did he want really? To go and see. To go so he wouldn't be sorry he hadn't. To go because it was all he had left, and he prayed it would stay alive. He wanted to reach the Forests, that was all.

And take Augustine to the sea.

But which way were the Forests?

In the middle of the city, Corentin looked at the ravaged streets and didn't know which way to go. He wandered for a long time without finding his way. Obeying some sort of insane impulse, or because it was the only way he knew, he went looking for the train station. The buildings, the clock towers, the train carriages had all collapsed, lay upon the rails, lay upon the people who'd been standing on the platforms. Corentin had believed in the lights and clamor of trains; he found nothing. Destinations were frozen on signboards.

So he followed track 7.

He didn't know what else to do.

Track 7 indicated, among other places, the name of the Little Town not far from the Forests. So he began to follow it.

* * *

It was a strange sensation to be walking along the empty, silent railroad tracks. Corentin frequently turned around: he thought he could hear a train. He would move a few steps to one side, not to be run over. But he was mistaken, no train came. So he went back to his place between the rails.

I'm the train, he thought.

He was tired already. The emotion had made him feel stiff all over, with an uncontrollable feverishness. The backpack on his shoulders weighed a ton. In the morning when he set out, he'd had something of a burst of energy: not from joy, not from excitement, nothing like the elation of leaving on vacation, but an urge to get going. A desire, a challenge. Fear, too, that he might find nothing but ash there, like here. But in his chest, a deep determination.

It wore off as the hours went by, with the miles, the heat.

When at midday he went through a first railroad station he climbed over the corpses that had fallen on the rails, not looking at them. Then he left the rails and went into the little town. He needed something to drink. It was both terrible and wonderful: he could just help himself. All he had to do was go into a shop and reach for a bottle. Instinctively, he touched the wallet in his pocket, but there was no need to pay. All he had to do was put the water in his pack and go back out, vaguely embarrassed.

It was here, in this town, that he saw the sign for the freeway. Here that he decided to follow the road rather than the tracks, and he left them for the melted, cracked asphalt.

In the end, it was easier to walk on the distorted pavement than on the ballast.

And besides, now that he had left the Big City behind, he knew the way.

Or only thought he knew the way.

Everything had changed.

But the road led to the Forests, that he knew. Even torn up and ravaged, even endless, it would take him there.

* * *

He spent the night in a shed next to a little house. In the main building he'd first gone into, the residents had been trapped by the thing, frozen in strange positions. He recoiled when he saw them. He tried not to let them enter his memory: the distressed bodies, the smell of death, the toys scattered on the floor. It had nothing to do with him. It wasn't his business. He had to force himself, steel himself.

There were only tools in the shed. Corentin lit a small fire with some twigs and took his time to go through them, choosing a knife and two big screwdrivers. He had found some cans of food in a cupboard and opened one at random rather than starting on his own supplies. It had no taste. He had to read the label to find out what it was (ravioli in tomato sauce). On the tiny flame of his fire the food hardly got warm, he forced himself to eat. It wasn't actually that the food was bland, it was that he had lost all sense of taste.

The night frightened him. The silence was terrifying: nothing but the dull tapping of the wooden spoon in the can, the crackling of the fire that went out quickly and that he had to keep feeding with bigger branches to have some light. But when he dozed off for an hour or two, or three, because he had no way of knowing, he was once again entirely on his own.

No stars, no moon, no hooting of owls. Predators would not come out. Prey would not be devoured. Nothing would happen that night.

Only solitude.

Something enormous, and the enormity was not nice.

Corentin expected to hear the muffled sounds of little nocturnal animals, wings unfolding, brief cries. He waited for the furtive passing of creatures, how they would slip through the darkness as they took a detour on discovering his presence.

He hoped.

He implored.

The night was empty.

* * *

He set off again the next day, his legs stiff from the miles he had walked and the weight of his backpack, and the silence buzzed in his ears as if there were an insect in there. The pavement gaped with long fissures, so Corentin walked along the edge. He looked to see how deep the crevices went—not actually that deep, they were more like wide irregular cracks. The soles of his shoes were sticky with tar, in places the road was still steaming. He wondered what could have burned everything like this and then he stopped wondering, he would rather not know, perhaps the vision of the melted roads, the burned bodies in cars that smelled of melted plastic and, already, of decomposing flesh: that was enough of an answer in itself.

When he came level with exit 3 of the four-lane highway, he remembered that by car the same distance from the heart of the Big City took half an hour.

And there was so much sadness as he walked through that landscape. In the blackened stalks of the vast fields of crops, in their charred ears, he could make out the wheat or barley that had been ready to be harvested. The trees looked like ghostly creatures, arms attempting a final gesture toward the heavens—but there were no more heavens, they were as gray as the ground, all borders had disappeared, too. Corentin followed the road and stopped looking for any horizon. He watched his shoes slowly moving forward. The blood was pounding in his temples, and there was no sound to drown it out, and so the drumming in his head was the only thing he heard. His eyes sank deeper into his face from fatigue.

He listened out for any sound, any movement.

But what could there be, on this deserted freeway, where the burned cars had entombed their drivers, where the fields were nothing but unending expanses as far as the eye could see, motionless, without life.

And what was the point.

If there was nothing left.

And yet, he thought again, when they had been underground, all six of them, they had made it, even if it was just luck. They had survived. And there were others—the two fugitives in the Big City. That was why he didn't give up on the Forests. That was why he didn't stop, didn't go back the way he had come, didn't return to the Big City for fear that the others, the five other survivors, would disappear completely.

Oh well.

They were no longer the ones he loved.

If the Forests were empty, then he would go back. There was always a chance.

What were fifteen more days, now that he had nothing to do?

Otherwise, he might as well just fall to the ground under the tall dead fir trees and stop moving. Lie there on a bed of needles. Like in the store two days ago (or was it even a day earlier), he would wait.

Maybe that would be the best thing.

He didn't have much strength.

He didn't really feel like it anymore.

A nd because these strange thoughts were pounding in his head, and fatigue was drumming in his ears, he did not hear the car coming.

He gave such a start when it blew its horn behind him—even though the horn had burned out and gave only a faint croak—that he fell over. He tripped on his own feet, his heart fit to burst. He had already grown used to wilderness. He scraped his leg all down the side.

Shit, shouted the driver apologetically as he climbed out. Are you all right?

Corentin didn't answer. He was looking at the car.

There was a car left—something that used to be called a car.

What is this, he said.

The driver scratched his head.

I have to leave it running, I'm not sure I'd get it started again.

But it's running.

For the moment, yes.

Corentin looked first at the car then at the driver, incredulously. It was as if they had emerged from a film, something completely impossible, totally off-beat, something that would have made him laugh had he felt up to it. The man was in his thirties. His brown hair was singed, and he had a bandage on his cheek. His shirt was buttoned all wrong. Corentin looked again at the car, its motor still running.

What is this, he said again—it was the only thing he could say and it was pointless.

I don't know. I tried every one of them at the entrance to the freeway. One after the other. I tried over a thousand. This one started. So I took it. The paint's melted and I still don't see how the electric wiring made it.

There are no tires.

No, there are no more tires.

So how do you manage.

I drive on the rims.

On the rims.

Yes.

They gazed pensively at the blistered car. Half the dashboard had oozed into long black ripples onto the floor.

Where are you going, asked the driver.

Corentin gave a broad, vague sweep of his arm into the distance.

That way.

I can take you.

Yes. Yes, why not.

I don't know how far. I don't know how much gas there is.

All right.

Since I'm driving on the rims I can't go fast. But it's better than nothing.

Better than nothing, yes.

Corentin walked around the car and pulled on the door handle. The door came off and fell with a clang of metal. He looked at it, taken aback. Then at the driver.

I'm sorry.

Don't worry. It isn't my car. Get in. There's no time to waste, while it's still running.

Corentin put his pack in the back and climbed into the sagging passenger seat. The driver gave a nod as he shifted into first gear.

I won't go fast. I'm driving on the rims.

* * *

They didn't go fast.

Scarcely any faster than on foot, perhaps.

But it wasn't as tiring, and there wasn't the burden of the pack across his shoulders.

Corentin shifted his sore legs this way and that. When he got stiff, he climbed out of the car and walked beside it for a hundred yards then got back in. The chassis swayed with his weight then settled again.

The rims grated along the pavement, the sound filling their ears.

They drove on the shoulder. In the other lanes they would have had to slalom their way continuously through the burned cars.

As long as they could, they didn't stop.

They didn't speak much. There would have been so much to say, from the cataclysm there before their eyes, to the tiny, ineffable luck they'd had of coming across each other and, for a few hours, not being alone on earth anymore. But they were in a state of shock. Corentin asked a few questions—when did it happen, how many days ago, how many had died, how many survived. The driver didn't know. The days were all mixed up, he couldn't tell one from the other anymore. He also didn't know why he had taken the freeway.

I figured this was the way to get out to the country.

His wife and children had died three floors above him in their building. The blast had gone over while he was repairing a water leak in the basement. That was what had saved him. Only him, on his own. No one was waiting for him in the country. He was just going there because he couldn't stay in the town next to his dead wife and children. But that was all in the past now.

I have to look ahead, he said.

Corentin was looking ahead too, through the missing windshield. It was all a question of point of view. They might have been in a beach buggy driving to the seaside, their hair streaming in the wind—or in the desert: Corentin had dreamt of going to the desert in Morocco someday.

It's all too sudden, he murmured.

It's in the past, said the driver again.

As they drove, scraping along on the rims at a few miles an hour, he pointed to the stony ground and charred vegetation as they went by.

That's the past. You see, it all disappeared behind us. And this too is the past. Corentin turned around to look more closely at the upturned truck the driver was pointing to.

The past. No point even thinking about it anymore.

After that they fell silent. Corentin was thinking of the Big City, in ruins, an entire world that had been wiped out, nothing left. And then he stopped thinking: shattered by emotion and the bad night he'd spent, he fell asleep, lulled by the rocking of the car as it juddered and moaned like a song, and he had the strange impression that for a brief moment he was safe, on the collapsed seat, with the electric wires tapping on his knees.

He opened an eye from time to time. Dangling from the driver's lips was a cigarette butt he'd found on the floor of the car. Corentin felt his head slump to the side again, it was all too heavy, he dozed off again. For a few minutes he forgot. There was nothing but the heat, the sound of the engine, the jarring of the road.

We're almost happy, said the driver at one point.

* * *

At the end of the afternoon, the car came to a halt. The driver turned the key in the ignition a few times with no luck.

That's it.

They sat there for a few minutes leaning against their seats, not speaking, eyes closed.

Right. This time, it's all over.

The rims smelled of heat, the blacktop sinking underneath them.

They climbed out. Corentin reached for his bag.

That was nice.

Which way are you headed, the driver asked again.

Corentin gave the same sweeping wave of his arm.

That way.

I could come along.

Yes.

There was a silence. They looked into the distance, the invisible horizon Corentin had pointed to. The driver nodded.

I think maybe I'll try to fix the car instead.

But it's run out of gas.

I'm going to try all the same.

All right.

Maybe I'll catch up with you.

Maybe you will.

The driver leaned over to open the hood. Corentin put his pack on his back and started walking again.

He walked until nightfall. He recognized the outline of a rest area in the distance. He knew he could find shelter to sleep there and some supplies. The ashen dust that covered everything was parching his throat. He had drunk too much. He wouldn't have enough water for the entire trip, he had to take some extra bottles, even if they were heavy.

He walked along the exit ramp, past a sign limiting the speed to thirty miles an hour.

He hesitated between the shop at the service station and the restaurants a little farther away. Finally, he decided on the shop.

Before he even went in, carefully avoiding the shattered door, he saw something move inside. His heart began to race.

Is anyone there.

Who's there.

And that's what he said:

Who is it.

They didn't answer. But he saw them.

They were piled up at the back of the store. They were lying on blankets and coats spread on the floor. There were six of them: two couples, and two children who were so dirty that no one would have been able to figure out who they belonged to or who they even looked like.

In a glance, Corentin understood.

They were dead.

They had deep burns on their faces, on their half naked bodies. They must have dragged themselves this far from their cars, thought Corentin. To wait for help, maybe. And then they succumbed to their injuries.

And yet, they had moved. He was sure of it.

In a quiet voice he called out, Hey.

He looked at their eyes. To see if they were turning toward him. But their eyes didn't move, didn't turn.

Corentin went closer. He kept an eye on the other doors, too. They were all closed.

With his foot, very cautiously, he nudged the man who was nearest.

Then it jumped with a cry. It happened so quickly Corentin didn't have time to do anything other than put his hands out in front of him.

Shit, he shouted.

Talk about a fright. Fucking cat.

What are you doing here.

The cat was a tabby, a black and ginger alley cat. It stopped still and looked at him from its hiding place behind a display. It was waiting for Corentin to leave.

You want me to open the door?

The cat didn't move. It was looking at the dead people.

Hey, murmured Corentin.

Don't you go eating those kids, hear?

But of course it would—since there was nothing else.

So Corentin took two blankets and rolled the children up inside. He dragged them over behind one of the doors and closed it. He almost threw up from the smell.

Shit—children, he said, wiping his tears.

They're not supposed to die at that age.

* * *

There were dead people in the big building next to the shop, too.

They deserve a burial as well, thought Corentin. Millions of graves to dig. A lifetime of burying people.

And who would dig a grave for him, at the end?

* * *

All things considered, the dead were not the worst.

You got used to the dead. Even the smell became familiar, like when you lived next to a tannery or a slaughterhouse. It was unpleasant but familiar. And then there was the astonishment and consolation of still being alive, and the distance you gained as you walked past the corpses: it's not me, it's not me.

The dead people were someone else, and someone else, Corentin couldn't give a fuck. He forced himself. There was no room for being sorry, he had to keep his strength for himself. The omnipresence of the dead made them ordinary. They were everywhere, there were too many of them, they were all the same. Climbing over them in stores, at gas stations—it had become banal.

No, the worst was all the rest.

But there was nothing left, so the rest meant what was absent.

A void of people, animals, forests, noise, movement. All gone, the tall trees and the motionless road, the cars, the rumbling of engines. Devoured—people, voices, laughter, shouts.

In the charred landscapes, on the motionless road.

In the solitude and silence.

It was enough to make you lose your mind a thousand times over.

And the strange absence of color.

Everything was gray. Corentin looked up at the sun that no longer rose; it was an unending half-night, a perpetual dawn. A dust of ashes blocked the sky.

His eyes went mad, hoping for color. Waiting for brilliance, spots, sparks. Looking for light. They saw the same thing everywhere. The grayness eventually scorched his eyes.

His brain went mad.

His hands went mad—one day of despair he looked at them, put them around his neck and tried to strangle himself.

It had to stop. He'd overestimated himself. He had believed he was stronger than he actually was.

He squeezed, squeezed tighter. Poor dream. He couldn't.

The pressure decreased and he coughed, gasping. His arms fell to his sides.

He was alive.

He began to weep.

The only color was the color of blood.

Corentin noticed this when he cut his hand on a piece of wood one night while making a fire. The blood flowed onto his palm, then onto his fingers. To his reeling mind, these were the colors of autumn, flamboyant, gleaming ruby, incandescent with an unbelievable vermilion. Blood reflecting the vanished sun.

He gazed at it in wonder.

He realized that it didn't exist, before.

Now he knew how to create color. He carried it inside him. In spite of all the misfortune, the thing had not been able to destroy what he had inside.

It wasn't faith.

Or his soul.

But the color red.

The blood.

Sometimes, along the freeway, he would jab his skin with the tip of the knife to be sure it was still there. Two or three scarlet drops. He gave a soft laugh as he looked at them.

When he stopped to eat, he cut himself on purpose on the rims of food cans.

He scratched at the cuts so they wouldn't heal. When he pressed on them, there was always a little blood that came out. There was something immortal, deep inside him. It was infinite.

It wasn't just his eyes, or his head, or his hands anymore.

Everything inside him was going insane.

* * *

The disappearance of colors, and the silence.

The silence left him with his mouth open, his arms open—horrified.

It was as if he'd gone deaf, and he rubbed his ears so hard they hurt: to bring them back to life, to hear something again.

But he wasn't deaf.

It was just that all sound had vanished, too. There was nothing to hear.

All he could hear were his own sounds: his shoes on the road, the rasping of his breath, his muffled moans. The lid on the cans he opened. The wrapping on the bread or cookies he found in rest areas, the bottles of water squeaking against each other in his pack. The depth of his voice trying to sing to fill the space, too vast.

And that was all.

When he was silent, when he stopped, when his breathing fell quiet: there was nothing left.

Just the strange rustling inside his head, like the one you hear when you hold a seashell up to your ear, thinking it's the sea you can hear inside.

That, and his pulse throbbing and pounding—in his chest, his belly, his head, his temples. Sometimes it kept him awake at night. He could toss and turn every which way: that heavy, deep pulsing shook right through him, with tiny vibrations. He blocked his ears and then the beating of his heart went through his hands, electrifying his fingertips, squeezing his body.

He hummed.

Very quietly.

The sound resounded in his head, grew unbearable. He stopped. He strained toward the world and waited.

The cry of a bird, the scuttling of a field mouse through the leaves.

In the distance, the hum of a tractor, voices calling.

Nothing, nothing.

He hadn't gotten out of the habit yet, he still listened.

It was all in vain.

It was all futile.

* * *

Despite his exhaustion, he didn't sleep much. He was still afraid.

That something might come again.

He woke up a dozen times during the night, thinking he'd heard a rumbling, a roll—thunder, or the earth. At any sign of trembling, he put one hand on the ground to make sure, and nothing fluttered under his palm. His throat was dry. He spat black saliva.

He had assumed that as he left the Big City farther behind he would discover that the world was not entirely burned. He'd been wrong. The landscape still looked like lunar territory, not a blade of grass had survived, there was not a single leaf hanging from a tree. It was still the same terrifying gray veil, the same uniformity.

If nothing grew anymore, what would he eat in a year or two, when he'd used up every can of food in every city? Who or what would he have to fight in order to live a few weeks or a few months longer—even though, and he already knew this, he would want only one thing and that would be to die, too, it was just that it would come when it came, it wasn't up to him to decide, he didn't have the nerve.

That bloody instinct that would never let go.

That bloody hope, which would never fade.

But he'd figure it out later.

For the moment, he had to sleep, and he wasn't sleeping. He had to rest, and rest eluded him, consuming him bit by bit, wearing him down, with short spells where he nodded off for fifteen minutes.

He often thought he heard someone coming. But it was always an illusion.

He hadn't seen anyone since the driver four days earlier, or five, or six. And he'd started keeping track of the passing days on a notepad, because he'd already lost count up to that point. He had thought he'd never forget those days of chaos. But now everything was constantly the same. Everything had lost so much of what made for difference. Yesterday or the day before or the morning before that. So now he wrote a date every night when he stopped, maybe he had one day too many or not enough, because he wasn't sure of the count he'd made for the first days after the thing. It didn't really matter. He just wanted to keep track of how much time had gone by since the end of the world.

How much time he would hold out.

But when he thought that maybe one day he would be counting in terms of years, he started to tremble.

Years all alone.

He no longer believed Augustine might still be alive. He hadn't seen much life since he set out. He pursued his journey the way you do a dream, or a quest—knowing they are impossible but that it is equally impossible to abandon them, because they are all you have left.

We'll find out later, he kept telling himself.

We'll find out when we get there.

He didn't say *I*. It was too hard. He would rather share his disappointment—but there, too, with whom, with what.

It was probably a stupid idea to have followed the freeway, because he didn't go through any villages or towns. He'd squandered his chances of finding survivors along the way. But it was the only way he knew.

He didn't have any other ideas.

He was tired.

H e'd had to jog his memory to recognize exit ramp 22 from the twisted signpost; the paint had run in the heat. The number was illegible unless you knew what to look for. But then Corentin spotted the little mound level with the ramp, which in fact he had gone beyond, and then the two tight bends.

He went back.

This was it. This was the road that led to the Forests.

Well, not quite yet, there were still nearly a hundred miles to go, if he remembered correctly. But this was where he had to leave the freeway, otherwise he'd end up too far south. Now he would have to change direction, head southeast. He'd have to take the back roads, cross country, through the villages, woods, and forests.

But first.

He took the notepad where he wrote down his dates, and a few landmarks, or things that struck him. He counted: nine days since he'd left—but nine days was unthinkable for such a distance, so long, so heavy on his back, he'd been dragging his feet; besides, he hadn't left the Big City right away.

After he thought about it, he crossed the dates out and added what seemed to make more sense: an additional day.

Crossed them out again, because he'd forgotten the day in the car, and the hours he might have gained. He thought: so, it could be.

But how much time in the car, how many miles gained?

He drew a huge oval on a fresh sheet of paper. Inside it he wrote: nine days, more or less. He started over.

He stared at the blank sheets on the notepad.

What if he reached the end, one evening? If there could be that many days after the end of the world.

There was room for at least four thousand lines.

More than ten years.

Would the end of the world last ten years? He put the notepad away, banishing the thought, his hands trembling, a sinking feeling in his chest.

He started walking.

* * *

For the first time, he went through the toll booth by walking around it. He thought: for the last time, too, no doubt.

A bit farther along he gazed at the tall metallic buildings that had gone up ten years earlier, offices and warehouses that had been a reddish-brown color you could no longer see. Now they were flows of black and gray steel, twisted girders reaching into the void and curling back on themselves, sheets of metal welded by who knew what force. In the parking lot the hundreds of cars resembled dead birds.

It began to rain.

* * *

It began to rain and all at once he experienced a sort of wild joy on feeling the water on his body, on seeing the grayness of the sky gradually diminish as it grew lighter and long dirty streaks formed on the ground. He felt the rain viscerally: it was salvation. It would cleanse the earth, it would go beneath the crust, beneath the rock if need be, to seek out what it needed to get the world going again, the last seeds, the last germinations, whatever embryos of life might have been spared.

Water: for so long he'd been hearing how rare it was becoming, that there was no longer enough of it to heal the seasons of drought—now the water had come. He didn't really need it, but he was glad to see it still existed. At that moment it was more precious than a heap of diamonds.

Water and light, for the world to begin again.

Corentin pressed his hands on his gut, the emotion was too raw. He lifted his face to the sky, drowning his tears in the rain, spreading his hands, and he began to laugh.

One minute. Perhaps two.

The time it took to feel the burning.

He wiped his eyes in a gesture of terror, and spat out the rain.

The water was burning.

His tongue, his cheeks, his skin.

His eyelids were already red.

He cried out, looked for a place where he could rinse himself off—there was nothing anywhere, and the thought overwhelmed him, everything must have been contaminated, all the lakes, all the ponds, all the puddles were burning.

Water had become poison.

He took a bottle from his pack and splashed his face, sheltered beneath the metal sheeting of a big building that had collapsed. He was trembling. The thought came to him in a flash: what if he too began to melt, devoured by this liquid that was infiltrating everything.

It took him a long time to dare to go back out, to dare to set off again in the unceasing rain. In the big warehouse, he found some tarps which he wrapped around himself like a long coat, protecting his pack and cloaking his rain jacket, which was no longer waterproof, ruined by the acidity of the rain.

It horrified him to see how everything was corroded by this

toxic water, how everything was lined with strange white streaks, all the color washing away, and on his hands and arms, in spite of the tarp and his precaution, his skin too became streaked. He kept his sleeves pulled long and hid his face from the rain.

That evening he spat on the rashes that had surfaced, even though no light, no sun had shone on him.

That night he couldn't fall asleep. He understood that the world was not being reborn after the cataclysm, and that the tragedy was ongoing, perhaps getting even worse, like an irrepressible force unleashed at full speed and which no amount of wanting could appease; those who had died had known the sweetness of escape—an escape from the slow disintegration of a world that had begun to eliminate the living, one individual after the other, down to the very last one.

* * *

The wind rose.

If Corentin was walking in a southeasterly direction as he should, that meant the wind was due south.

He held the tarp out over his head to shelter from the relentless drizzle. He got wet no matter what, it seeped in everywhere, he was seized by damp.

At the end of the day his feet were soaked, and his shoes had split open on the side. His skin was burning, he shivered with both fever and cold.

He made a fire at the edge of a barn, sufficiently sheltered to dry his things but just outside enough not to set everything on fire. He opened his cans of food one after the other. He ate without thinking, the same thing every day, because he'd given up on vegetables, which didn't provide enough energy and left him with his guts growling and a bitter taste in his mouth. He had cans of ravioli, lentils, and sausages. And bottles of water.

He often went into the houses he passed on the way. In the beginning, he would call out. Did he really still believe someone would answer? He didn't dare open the door without warning.

He went straight to the kitchen.

It was crazy, he'd noticed, how much time people spent in their kitchens. Half the bodies were in the kitchen.

He'd stopped looking at them.

He saw them well enough, it didn't affect him anymore. There were too many and he couldn't do anything for them, it was no longer a time for pity.

He walked past them to reach the cupboards and he took jars, flour, fruit in syrup, jams. The taste of sugar brought him a fleeting comfort. When he opened a jar of cherry plums or strawberries, he pictured the orchards as they used to be, the abundant gardens, the careful harvests.

He immediately went back out to settle into a shed, a workshop, or a barn.

He saw nothing that he recognized in this world.

It rained for three days.

E ven the fire could no longer warm him. His clothes would not dry out. He became resigned to moving bodies so that he could sleep in a real house, in a real living room, by a burning fireplace sheltered from drafts. He had already grown unaccustomed to living between four walls. The sensation of enclosure terrified him. What if the house began to collapse around him or he was trapped by God knows what, and there was no way out; what if an ember fell on the carpet during the night. The safety of houses came back to him slowly, with a fleeting sense of comfort.

On the third day of rain, he didn't move. The sight of the ravaged sky at dawn got the better of him. He stayed flat on his back all morning, only getting up to put some wood on the fire.

He slept.

It was not a restorative sleep but an exhausting one, full of nightmares and fear, of sudden starts awake, of dozing off all too briefly.

He had a fever.

He had visions.

For the first time since the end of the world he went looking for alcohol, and drank it strong and quickly, to fall, to founder, for the forgetfulness to come.

When he awoke, he was shivering on the sofa and the fire had gone out. He had completely lost his bearings.

It was daylight outside—but was it afternoon, or almost evening?

Was it the next day?

On his notepad he added an extra day.

Maybe.

Then he ate, gathered his belongings, and left.

* * *

Eight or ten miles farther along he came to the first forests.

Entire hillsides of blackened trees and he looked at them without shuddering; he had grown used to this, too.

It was just that he saw them. He didn't nod, didn't say anything.

Not: these forests have burned, too.

Not: these forests that were so old and grand.

He didn't have any particular thought. He glanced at them, registered the information with a sort of resigned distance, and continued along the shrunken roads.

It was more difficult now that the meadows and fields had been replaced by the woods, because with the impact of the thing and of the wind and rain, a lot of trees had fallen across the road. Corentin was constantly having to walk around them, they were too tall, too tangled to climb over.

He entered dark, decimated labyrinths.

The air still smelled of fire.

It was at the end of one of the uprooted trees that the sound came to him.

He could not believe it.

Blasting apart the silence, with a sound so tiny.

He stopped and listened.

But this time, there was something. There really was something.

Something so sad that he froze, something so mournful that for a moment he hesitated to go and see.

Maybe it would be better to keep going.

It was weeping.

Whimpering.

Corentin squeezed his hand over his heart. There was someone.

But who. And in what sort of a state.

Instinctively, he spun around to keep on going. He didn't want to know. He'd seen enough misfortune on the road, he wasn't sure he could take it anymore.

He fled.

A few feet.

Then he ran back. This was crazy, this was stupid.

Get out of there.

There was someone.

But who.

He was short of breath. The fatigue, the panic.

He broke a branch to clear the way, stepped forward, stopped. He couldn't hear it anymore. No, no, it couldn't have disappeared. He put it like a question:

Who's there.

Oh the sob, the cry, the call.

Get out of here, said a voice inside.

He began running. He took his knife in his hands. Even though the leaves had burned, and the grass was gone, he could see nothing.

Or else it was the fear. A veil before his eyes.

All of a sudden, he found them.

* * *

Corentin fell to his knees. And, either from disappointment or relief that the weeping sound was not human, he let out a long cry.

It must have been days. Days that it had been pounding

inside him, and he'd let nothing out, because he mustn't weaken. Mustn't give way. And it had all accumulated inside him like indigestion, like some rot that just kept on piling up— at last, it all came out in tears that drowned out the whimpering of the dogs lying there in front of him, huge tears, and for a moment the animals were silent.

Yes, for a moment they made no sound.

Then they began again to sob, because they didn't know what else to do. Because they were too young. They were lying at their dead mother's side, they must have been waiting for her to wake up, for days and days, as their strength ebbed away, their mouths open for the milk that didn't come.

And bit by bit, Corentin's cries stopped, and he could not take his eyes off the trembling little bodies.

There were six puppies. They could no longer stand and were lying one on top of the other, atrophied, defeated. It was too late.

They were dying.

Corentin understood this the moment he drew near, between the end of his sobs and his tears. The puppies paid him no attention—it was too hard for them even to turn their heads. He picked one of them up, it closed its eyes for a second and it died.

The others were there as if waiting.

So Corentin, his tears never stopping, killed them.

All of them, one after the other.

It was nothing. It was just dogs.

It was a deliverance.

But deep inside him, he felt terrible.

* * *

Sitting next to seven bodies, the six puppies and their mother.

Something had snapped inside him.

He stroked them with his fingertips. They were still warm.

Corentin didn't want to get to his feet.

And who would finish him off to set him free? If he prayed. If he begged.

There were no more tears. The forest closed over the silence.

* * *

And then behind a tree he saw it, on its way back, staggering, the last puppy.

The seventh one.

The one that wasn't there a moment ago, and now it was coming toward him like an apparition.

T he puppy came and sat clumsily between Corentin and its dead siblings. There were sores all over its body—from brambles, bites, burns.

It stood there at the edge of the world, saying nothing.

What are you doing?

The puppy raised its white eyes to him.

It was blind.

Oh, sighed Corentin.

And suddenly it was more then he could handle. He tried to find a reason not to kill it too, this puppy sniffing the bodies, not whimpering, not weeping.

Does it know I'm here? wondered Corentin after a moment.

The puppy hadn't moved. It was still sitting there. Corentin liked its calm manner, the way it looked straight ahead without seeing a thing—the way it pretended.

Are you hungry?

Corentin opened a can, offered the puppy food and drink, and it ate and drank. Then it climbed onto his lap and fell asleep, and Corentin didn't dare to move for fear of waking it.

* * *

You coming, Blind Boy?

They set off together into the mist.

The puppy sniffed the air, sniffed the lifeless bodies near him. For the first time, he let out a plaintive moan.

I'm sorry, murmured Corentin.

The little creature looked toward the voice, sneezed, then fell in step behind him without turning around.

* * *

Because it was too young and too weak, Corentin took the puppy in his arms. Otherwise, he would constantly have to wait for it. It couldn't walk very well. It drifted off. Corentin had to guide it with his voice, watch it closely, sometimes he had to go and get it, when it got stuck among the branches and couldn't get out.

He could have left it in the woods, not to be burdened with a companion that wasn't worth much and didn't look particularly hardy—probably, if he'd run off into the forest, the puppy would never have found him. More than anything, Corentin was afraid he'd come upon him stiff and lifeless one morning, and he was afraid of sorrow.

But it was the only life left.

He clung to it, suddenly, as to a lifeline.

As he held the puppy close, he thought about how this was the first warmth he had felt since the end of the world—that of a blind and damaged puppy—and in the next village he stopped in the pharmacy, because he'd never thought he might need some medication. He treated the animal, and pocketed all the painkillers and antibiotics that were left.

* * *

Corentin continued along the road even though night was falling.

In his mind he had to keep going, bravely, relentlessly, to get to the Forests, as if the Forests meant salvation, as if they might have been spared. He knew it was impossible.

And he thought, so what.

I have to get there.

He urged himself on in a low voice.

Hey, I have to get there.

With this great illusion. Just to gain some time.

Wedged on his shoulders, the puppy pretended to gaze out at the landscape through the drifts of fog. Corentin could feel its warm body next to his.

They came to the next village in the middle of the night. It was so completely dark, and the moon was so entirely absent, that Corentin could only make out the road from the sound of his shoes on the pavement. Every ten steps or so he would drift off to the side, and then he heard the dull sound of his soles on something soft—scorched grass or ashen earth, and he turned off and came back, holding his arms out ahead of him to avoid bumping into a tree or a signpost.

Blind Boy's paws around his neck brought him some comfort.

There were the two of them. They were all on their own.

They collapsed in the first barn they found. Corentin forced himself to make a fire and eat, and shared a can of ravioli with the puppy. He was exhausted. But he felt less sorrowful than on previous nights.

For the first time, there was some color—Blind Boy's blemished beige coat.

And there was sound: the animal's panting as it shook itself, its faint yapping as Corentin brought the food closer, and the puppy would begin frantically chewing, dipping his nose in the sauce up to his jowls.

It isn't much, thought Corentin looking at the puppy. A pretty meager consolation, a blind dog. But in this new configuration, with a world emptied of its occupants, any form of life was a source of joy. He hoped the dog would recover from its wounds and its emaciation, at least that, if it didn't regain its eyesight. Corentin pictured himself carrying the puppy in his arms for its entire life, hoped it wouldn't get too heavy, and at the same time he wanted the scrawny little creature to become a big strong animal, like a giant cuddly toy that would protect him—in his dreams.

But wasn't there something of a dream, or a nightmare, in what had happened, and wasn't everything imaginable permissible from now on? They fell asleep side-by-side under the damp blanket.

* * *

The pond was covered with dead fish. They examined it for a long time. Blind Boy, leaning forward on his paws, tried to touch the silver belly of a roach or a carp. Corentin pulled him back—the thing had poisoned the water.

We can't eat them.

The puppy tried again all the same, and Corentin picked him up off the ground and held him close.

From a distance, he had thought he could see thousands of sparkling lights, he couldn't make them out clearly, but they seemed cheerful and luminous. A shimmering. Life beneath the surface of the water, slowly moving: that was how he imagined the fish, their carefree existence disturbed only, when they were not well hidden, by the fearful figure of a fisherman, and then everything became a flashing of tails, everything rushed down to the silty bottom and disappeared. Corentin had believed there might be schools of living fish, it really looked like there could be. But it was only their scales, still shining, the scales of thousands of alevin, of roach the size of a hand, or millennial carp, their silver soon to tarnish. In two or three days, the pond would be nothing but a vast expanse, gray and squamous.

When the winds turned, the smell was already vile.

Wherever they went, they always ended up with the foul smell in the air, it came from fish, it came from people, it came from the world. The stench had descended upon them. Corentin recalled the butchers' trucks that used to come for the dead animals in the Forests, before: cows, calves, goats, sheep, occasionally a horse; a whiff of fetid air always followed. He would hold his breath, it smelled of rotting flesh, there was no other word for it, and that's what it was, piles of carrion, and that is what the earth smelled like.

Now there were no more trucks, but the smell was the same. Everywhere. All the time. With every step they took, Corentin and the puppy disturbed the soil and the effluvia was released, it emerged and clung to their skin. They stank of death, it had entered them, and as with all unspeakable odors, they could not smell it anymore.

* * *

That afternoon it snowed.

He was hardly surprised—there was no more room for surprise. It was a sort of resigned despair. The rain hadn't stopped, they were making their way covered by the tarp (Corentin had cut out a square to partially protect the puppy); now the snow seemed to him a possible way of going on.

Even when Corentin gave a long sigh and wiped his face— it was the end of July.

Nothing surprised or frightened him.

Anything could happen now.

The temperature had been dropping abnormally since morning, they'd been shivering in the rain.

It began to snow, they said nothing, they just looked.

Then they hunched over.

This was so different from previous years, which had merely gotten hotter then hotter still, so different from that

warming everyone talked about and which had dried up half
the trees and half the creatures. Corentin thought about the
heat in the catacombs, the stifling air, how their skin had
pearled with sweat. He was not used to cold anymore. In winter it used to rain but didn't freeze. This snow brought him
back to his very early years in the Forests, twenty years ago,
when Augustine had shown him how to make a snowman, how
to decorate it with a carrot for a nose and pebbles for eyes and
how to put a pipe in its mouth, a pipe he'd never seen her use
for any other purpose. It had lasted for two or three seasons,
then the snow stopped, and never came back.

Except now, in July.

Blind Boy asked to climb into Corentin's arms and he hid
beneath the cloak, as if he were burying himself in a den to get
away from the strange, thick rain. Corentin could no longer see
the desolate countryside. He didn't notice the shrinking horizon that came crashing right into them, wrapping the rest of
the world in a faded halo that no gaze could penetrate. Now
the future was uncertain thirty feet ahead, the road submerged
in whiteness. Because of the wind the snowflakes were stinging; in order not to swallow them he had to keep his mouth
closed, however tired or breathless he might feel. Solitude had
never been more palpable. To Corentin it was as if all he had
to do was reach out his hand and he could touch it.

He kept his arms wrapped close, gripping the tarp to hold
it in place, to hold on to the puppy. The plastic sheet flapped
against his legs. The snow melted when it landed there, then
trickled downward: his trouser legs were soaked. The stiff,
frozen cloth against his skin—he walked faster, so his teeth
wouldn't chatter, so he wouldn't shiver all through his body. As
if his blood had deserted him.

He was the color of snow, white inside.

Damp.

Cold.

But Blind Boy could not see any of that; he had fallen asleep.

The dog didn't wonder which was falling faster, the snow or the night. He was not enduring the icy hours, he was not looking for a hamlet, a house, a ruined barn where they could stop at last, at the edge of the dark forests.

He was not thinking to himself, for even a few seconds, that the footprints Corentin left as he walked through the powdery snow were, until they were covered over, the only living thing in the world, and the only sign that the living still existed.

He woke up when he felt the heat from the fire. He was lying on a little bed of straw. Next to him Corentin was trembling, his hands held out over the flames as he tried in vain to get warm. And already, the fever.

At first, he thought he was dreaming

In his dream, the world was breaking up, cracking apart. He couldn't identify where the sound was coming from, he couldn't see anything—it was nighttime. But that's what it was: everything was cracking.

Like the sound of a boat's hull splintering.

The sound of a frozen lake where the ice is gradually fissuring into thousands of crystal shards.

The sound anything might make under pressure, as it gives way and breaks.

It really was the trees.

Corentin woke up with a start. The day was just dawning. Blind Boy, gazing vacantly into space, was baying at the absent moon.

* * *

The snow was snapping the trees.

Months of drought, and suddenly the wind. And suddenly the cold, the terrifying frozen weight on the tree trunks and the charred leaves still hanging from the leafstalks.

The branches were shattering like glass.

Corentin moved further back into the barn. They were surrounded by forest, and the forest was falling. His eyes were open wide, incredulous. And yet.

He could hear the cracking increase in momentum, then

end with a dull clatter, as wooden limbs clashed and smashed against each other. The trees tried to resist. They clung exhaustedly to their branches down to the last fiber. In vain: all of them fractured, in the end, their branches torn off as the trunks split in two and cracked down to the ground.

Shreds of bark dangled from the branches of those trees still standing. One by one the branches broke off. They crashed to the ground with a vibrant sound, a dull explosion.

Every twenty seconds. Corentin counted to forget his fear. Every twenty seconds something shattered.

The barn roof echoed as the trees fell, split open on one side. Every time, the structure trembled, swayed unsteadily, as if uncertain. The walls seemed to expand with each blow, the cracks grew wider as the building shook. One more blow and everything would collapse.

The blow came. The barn still stood.

If Corentin and the puppy had been outside, they would have been crushed. Not a single space escaped the strange bombardment; not a patch of earth was safe from the stakes that pierced the air and landed in the ground, straight as arrows, proud as pickets.

Will this ever stop? Corentin implored silently.

It lasted for at least two hours.

Two hours to amputate hundreds or thousands of trees, leaving only a forest of useless, bare trunks, bony outlines that could no longer welcome anything, neither birds nor insects nor dust. In some places, broad-leaved or coniferous trees had fallen all the way to the ground, uprooted. The branches lay at their feet, like corpses on a battle field. But there had been no battle.

And two hours, that wasn't a storm.

It was an eternity.

* * *

Corentin didn't know what had made him sick—the cold or the devastation, viruses that should have all died, or fear.

But he was sick.

And he knew only one thing: he could not afford to be sick. At present, there was only life or death—nothing in between or halfway, no half-measures, no compromise.

So which side was he headed for?

In spite of the medicine, the fever persisted.

He had to get up. He had to hit the road, keep going—not moving was halfway to death. He had to get up, even though his head was spinning like a top, his body was seized with shivering, and his stomach was queasy. His legs were like jelly, he was sure he would fall. He didn't fall. He continued on his way, on course, although his vision was blurred, and the sweat seemed to freeze on his brow, and his back couldn't take it anymore, trying to stand up straight, racked with pain. He was dying of heat and shivering. He stopped a dozen times. His trembling and shortness of breath would not let him take another step. He bent double. He knelt on the snow that was melting a little to try and catch his breath—not to lose consciousness, he was dead scared that he might, he felt himself drifting away, he tried to calm his panic-stricken breathing. When the malaise had ebbed enough, he set off again. Ten yards and everything came back. The pain in his eye sockets, the blood pounding in his head, the dizziness. His entire body was pleading for mercy. He resisted. Even Blind Boy, with his little puppy paws, could walk better than he did.

He would preserve a confused vision of that day, when he wanted to get back on the road, the impossible memory of the huge game of pick-up sticks there before him. There was no more road. It was buried under an endless pile of shattered timber. He could see where the road led for a few yards—and then it disappeared, swallowed by the black and gray wood. He tried to clear a path. He tried to weave his way. The branches grabbed hold of him, constantly held him back, clinging to his arm or his coat, creating an inextricable lattice-work which forced him to turn back. He could not discern an end to the strange chaos. As far as the eye could see, the forest was blocking any way through.

And so, he went around.

He started up the slope. He climbed for nearly an hour. He could hardly breathe, he kept his mouth wide open to take some air into his burning throat. He had taken Blind Boy in his arms for a while, then put him back on the ground. The puppy whimpered—Corentin didn't have the strength to carry him. Eventually he sat on the ground, right in the snow, it was stu-pid, he'd get soaked. But he couldn't think anymore. All his strength went into his struggle to breathe, into his pulse pounding clear to his temples, making his head, even his eyes, feel as if they were about to burst.

He took another aspirin.

He should have stopped, looked for shelter, made a fire.

Later.

He just wanted to get out of the labyrinth.

And in any case, there were no more houses, no more barns, nothing.

When his heartbeat would let him, he set off again. It took him two more hours to circumvent the devastated forest and find the road again.

The sign indicated the name of the village with the figure 3 next to it. Three miles—that was too far. Corentin looked at the tired dog by his feet, holding one paw in the air.

Too far for both of them.

But did they have any choice?

If we can find a hut, we'll stay the night there.

There were no huts. There was only the shattered road and his legs about to collapse from carrying and walking. The straps of the backpack were sawing his shoulders, he dreamt of throwing out all the cans and water bottles one after the other, until he could no longer feel the weight on his back, or the bloody rubbing just below his shoulder, or the squeezing sensation between his shoulder blades, there was no point shaking his arms and his body, the shoulder straps always ended up back in the same place, and the muscles would seize up all over again.

Fuck, he said.

Not in anger, in exhaustion.

It felt as if his shoes were sinking into the asphalt with every step he took. He turned around to look. No, there was nothing but slush.

Or else it was his bones colliding, collapsing into each other from the effect of exhaustion and the weight he was dragging around to survive, an entire house, and yet the most important thing was always missing.

His entire body was in pain. It had been going on too long.

He hadn't been ready. No one was ready for this.

Inside his shoes, there was blood. At night he'd stopped taking them off because whenever he did a little bit more skin came off with them. His skin was red, white, and yellow—and his socks, too, were red, white, and yellow. He would rather not see. He simply loosened the laces to relax the grip. He wasn't cold that way. Before the fever.

Or before the snow.

Where was he, now, on this terrible journey?

He knew: three quarters of the way.

But this no longer made him feel better. There was no more power in it.

He kept on going, prey to a sort of delirium.

He was barely shuffling, no length to his stride. One foot.

More than that and his legs began to falter. He was a hundred years old.

He was a thousand years old—when he told himself the world was dead and that he was going on for nothing, going nowhere, basically, and that he must never stop.

Of course, that was impossible. He would stop. He could see very clearly how it would come to him, the last instant: fatigue, his eyes bulging, he would falter and then, because sooner or later the end would come—he would fall. The last time. He would have no more energy, no more reserves to pull himself back up. Before, he would never have believed this. Before, he thought this only happened to horses who are driven too far.

But the lack of strength, now. He knew.

He was convinced he could fall by the side of the road and die there because he had no resistance left. Not even the slightest urge to try: just a breath. Faint. That was all. One last round then say farewell. He'd be dead.

And afterwards.

And Blind Boy.

Corentin looked frantically for the puppy. Couldn't see him, and he realized that it was almost dark, he hadn't noticed the darkness, it was a slightly deeper shade of gray, he didn't give a damn. But now it was nighttime and Blind Boy was not there. He didn't call to him. In the end, he would rather be alone.

He knelt on the damp earth. His joints cracked, his legs hurt, his back ached. All he had left were sensations. Thought had vaporized. He had no more strength for that, either.

He would stop here. Collapse into a little pile by the side of the road.

Little piles like him—there were millions of them.

Blind Boy would go on his way. He'd manage. Dogs can eat anything.

Corentin lay down in the dirty melting snow. On his hair, in front of his eyes, snowflakes looked like mountains studded with stars. Night was settling in. That didn't change much, going from gray to black.

His heart was beating, somewhere deep inside. He waited to die.

Blind Boy yapped.

There he is, thought Corentin.

The puppy's bark wasn't right nearby. He'd gone on ahead. He yapped again.

Tearing himself from the earth, Corentin raised his head.

There was a light up ahead.

C orentin stared at the light for a long time without moving. Maybe he didn't understand.

In his world, light no longer existed.

And yet. He could see Blind Boy's puny shape on the road, standing out against a yellow square. The square was far away, partially obscured by the bony outlines of trees and groves, but it existed. Light had returned.

A single light.

Corentin stared at it, speechless, his eyes open wide. He knew he was still a long way from the Forests, from Augustine. He was on a little winding road at the edge of those hamlets which, even before the catastrophe, had been home to only a few elderly souls.

But there was a light. He wanted to laugh and cry at the same time. He couldn't take his eyes off that incredible, incongruous spot. He was completely mesmerized by its yellow glow. He had to get up. What if the light disappeared all of a sudden. Damn, he murmured, squeezing his fists against the ground to help himself up.

He tore himself from the earth and snow.

Only then, as he picked up his pack and staggered forward, did he feel the cold that had permeated his clothing.

* * *

He walked for a quarter of an hour, extremely slowly. He came to a village.

The light was in the village.

In a window.

Little light.

He stared at it the way you stare at a miracle.

He knocked at the door.

This was impossible.

This was like before.

An old lady came to open. He couldn't believe it.

Then he fell, the way he'd imagined dying. All at once, not knowing what hit him, because something inside had given way. It was exhaustion, suffering, despair.

And it was joy.

* * *

When he regained consciousness, he was still outside, on the threshold of the house. There was still a light inside. Someone had spread a blanket over him and closed the door again. He was freezing. His body was trembling, and he could not stop.

His voice was gone, when he wanted to cry out.

Please.

He waited, he didn't have the strength to call again.

And after a while, the door opened again.

You're awake, said the old lady, looking at him.

Awake?

I'm not strong enough to carry you in the house. I had to leave you outside.

A very old lady. Corentin squinted to try to see her more clearly.

Would you like to come in now?

I'm cold.

We made a fire.

So that's the light.

No. The light is from the candles.

* * *

It was warm. It smelled like soup. Blind Boy was asleep by the wood stove. On the other side of the stove, an old man sat all hunched up in an armchair. He didn't say hello, he didn't look up. He just mumbled something.

It's all the Krauts' fault.

Don't listen to him, apologized the old lady. He doesn't know what he's saying.

The old man bobbed his head up and down, over and over, like one of those cuddly toys people used to put in the rear window of their car. His hands were trembling the same way.

Corentin removed the tarp tied around his body and his wet coat.

The house was an old people's place, yellow and beige and brown. And there was also a slightly rancid smell that even the thing had not managed to eliminate completely; there was a tablecloth on a sideboard, and a figurine of the Virgin on a buffet. The table was set, the old lady hurried to add another place. It was as if nothing had managed to take hold. As if it had all passed them by—time, the shock wave, the catastrophe. Corentin looked around the room at the furniture, at the two old people. He didn't even know if—

Do you know what happened, he asked.

Yes. We saw.

Are there any other people here besides yourselves, I mean, people alive.

There's no one left.

I see.

We had a cat. But we haven't seen it since.

They ate in silence. There was a bit of bacon in the soup, and some toast.

It's good, said Corentin.

After the meal the old man returned to his armchair next to the stove and opened the newspaper he'd put down beside it. Corentin raised his eyebrows.

Are there newspapers?

It's two weeks old, explained the old lady. The last one we got. He reads it every evening.

I see.

He knows it by heart. At night he recites bits in his sleep.

I see.

And anyway, nothing more has happened since that day.

No. Nothing more has happened.

He can still read it, anyway. There's nothing new.

No. There's nothing new.

The old man grunted, creasing the newspaper.

It's all their fault, the Krauts.

You smell bad, whispered the old lady a little later, embarrassed.

And now that his body had warmed up and the cold was no longer mitigating the smell, Corentin had to admit it was true. It was even worse than that. He literally reeked. Even the puppy didn't stink like this.

It's been more than two weeks, he thought.

The same clothes. The same unwashed body. Water frightened him. It had become toxic, it burned. And besides, there had been no one to wash himself for, no one to tell him.

I'll get a washtub ready for you.

He immersed his dirty hair, his caked skin, smeared with greasy dust, ashes, filth. Finally, he put his feet in, with the socks sticking to his wounds, and he pulled the scabs off one by one. Then he disinfected them as best he could.

The old lady had placed clean clothes on a chair. He put them on, certain they had belonged to someone who was dead now. They smelled of lavender and they were soft.

When Corentin woke up, it took him a few seconds to remember where he was. The room didn't look like anything he knew. Only Blind Boy seemed familiar. Consciousness returned from a great distance, very slowly, unsure. He placed his hand on his brow: his fever had gone down.

The house smelled of coffee. This threw him, suddenly he was no longer sure of where he was. Neither the place, nor the era. Everything seemed normal again. Maybe he'd dreamt it all; but the thought stayed with him only briefly, he had slept in a house he didn't know, in the home of people he didn't know, and nothing was normal. It would just take time for hope to stop being instinctive and disappear.

He got dressed. The old lady was busy at the wood stove, which was also used to cook on. Pancakes were sizzling on the cast iron. At the back of the room, a door opened onto a pantry full to the rafters with supplies.

The old woman intercepted Corentin's sidelong gaze.

It was me. I went to take what I could find at the neighbors'.

A silence. Then she went on.

They'd all died, you see.

A few supplies, every day. Food and drink. Wood. Matches. Plastic bags. Clothes. Blankets. Pens and paper. Oil from garages. Everything, even things that seemed useless. Everything could be used. There were only twelve houses in the hamlet. The old lady had gone back and forth with her cart.

She gave a gentle laugh.

It was like shopping, a big shopping trip where you don't have to pay for anything. We've never had this much here before.

Corentin didn't ask her what it was for. He didn't say that even in a month or six or twelve, the time would eventually come when there'd be nothing left. But it was as if the old lady had read his mind.

Before, my husband kept a vegetable garden. Maybe he can go back to it. Maybe it hasn't all died.

Who knows.

* * *

He stayed all the next day with the old people. He went scavenging in the neighboring houses for everything the old lady hadn't been able to reach—whatever was too high or too low or too hard to carry. He brought back some new treasures, kept some of the food, and gave the rest to the old couple. Above all, he found a pump-action shotgun, almost brand-new; there were boxes of ammunition next to it on the shelf. The chamber took seven bullets.

A rifle could certainly come in handy. For game—but he knew very well that wasn't why he was taking it, because all the game was dead.

But maybe, if some came back.

No, he was lying to himself: it was for the living.

Sooner or later. He would have to defend himself, he would have to protect the little that had been restored to life.

Of course just then, in the beige house that smelled of soup and old people, Corentin thought that things would never get to that point. He thought that not everything had burned—

that much farther away, the world still existed the way it always had, and it was only a question of time before someone came to help them, to rescue them, to get basic things going again, like electricity and running water, like gas, transportation, agriculture. To him the situation was like the aftermath of war. They had to rebuild. Those who hadn't been affected would come. They would rebuild.

It would take Corentin years to lose hope.

For years, whenever something moved at the edge of the Forests, his heart would leap and his first thought would be: they've come.

Everything can begin again.

But it would turn out to be only a rock in the distance, falling from a cliff and rolling, or a tree creaking, or one of the rare birds that had reappeared and was perched unsteadily on a branch, half dead from hunger. Nothing whatever began again. The world had given up.

So, for the moment, Corentin tied the rifle to the side of his pack, and put the bullets inside among the cans of food. He stopped wondering why he had taken it. He was taking it, that was all. Fear had started forming terrible things in his head. And it wasn't so much about knowing whether he'd survive, since he had survived: it was a fear of the future.

Because from now on, one thing was sure, there would be a future.

And basically, maybe that was the worst thing there could be.

They'd been long, these last days. There was the accumulation—of miles, grayness, exhaustion. There was his growing fear, because it was no longer enough just to tell himself that Augustine was dead for him to feel ready. Corentin had lived with the assumption that if he thought about it often enough, he would get used to the idea, that it would seem obvious and normal. He had walked past thousands of corpses since leaving the Big City. It was trivial. That was just the way things were. He would glance at them the way you notice a hedgehog run over by the side of the road. There were so many: he could no longer be surprised. It had eventually begun to leave him indifferent.

But not Augustine.

He was attached to her, she was all he had in the world. In the Big City he had harbored illusions. He had lived with mirages, enacting deep friendships, sometimes love. There was nothing left of any of that. Everyone he'd known had cleared out, everyone had gone their own way. Had gone to find their loved ones. It still hurt when he thought about it.

Augustine, with her frowning air, her silent ways.

Augustine had always been there.

It was easy to go remembering it now that he was alone.

But there it was, he was on his way home.

Ninety-two years old. Good God, she was old. She was so very much older than old enough to die.

* * *

There was a sign.

One afternoon when Corentin, worn out, was walking with his eyes glued to the ground—it reduced the horizon, he didn't want to look too far, too far frightened him, he couldn't cope— one afternoon, there was a light at the toe of his shoe. And it wasn't a mistake, it wasn't a mirage, but a tiny blade of grass that had emerged from the dead earth, and the greenness of it almost hurt his eyes, so thoroughly had color vanished from the world. He crouched down to look at it. It was perhaps not quite an inch in length. He touched it with his fingertip, to be sure.

Maybe the old woman had been right.

Maybe not everything was dead, and the old man's vegetable garden would grow again.

For a moment he thought about picking the blade of grass, to prove to himself that it was really there. But it must have taken so much energy, so much determination for that little green shoot to grow there after the catastrophe, for it to find in its roots the strength to re-create something, to break through the earth and ash. He couldn't pull it up. That would be insane. He went on walking, filled with a sort of wild joy. Which departed with the onset of fatigue.

He was exhausted. Blind Boy was often on his back, wedged on top of the pack, his paws around his neck as usual, looking around. He could hear him breathing just next to his ear. There were times he wished the puppy would grow up all of a sudden in order to walk on his own. But there were other times when the creature's warmth against his skin calmed him.

Corentin had realized the puppy was not completely blind. He avoided trees, and road signs, and could make out large masses. He sniffed things. He listened. He actually managed pretty well. For sure, if he'd had to hunt for his food, it would have been tricky—there were times when, even though he paid attention, he would bump against something in the way, like a stone, or he'd stumble into a hole. He'd get up again and give himself a good shake. And off he'd go. He didn't give up.

On we go, thought Corentin, when he looked at him.

And he would adjust the pack on his shoulders, stretch his legs stiff with fatigue yet again, and follow Blind Boy.

* * *

Then there was that day when Corentin lost his nerve, going through a town, sitting on benches without seeing a thing, since there was nothing more to see. It used to be one of his favorite pastimes, before: sitting on a public bench and watching people. And now, there were still benches, with their blistered paint, but there was no one left to watch.

No more children running and shouting, no more old couples walking with their canes, adjusting their pace to their partner's. No more dogs, no more pigeons, no more smokers, no more students putting the world to rights—the world didn't want to be put right, and it had killed human life once and for all, just so it would finally be left alone.

An absolutely motionless wilderness. A sort of black-and-white postcard, frozen, soulless. Maybe a bit of wind would have blown the ash along the ground—the ash of trees, of dust, of humans.

There was no wind.

Maybe a bit of sunshine would have made everything burned less black and raw.

There was no sunshine.

Corentin got up from the last bench at the end of the afternoon and continued on his way.

He wanted to leave the useless benches of towns behind.

Leave the cloying effluvia he recognized only too well: the scarf tied over his nose and chin was not enough. He had no idea how long the stench would last. Once, at Augustine's place, a house marten had died in the roof. The stench of carrion had lasted for nearly six months. The cold will freeze it, Augustine had said, at the beginning. In the spring, when she noticed the smell again, she shook her head: the summer heat would dry it out. In the end they had to wait for the worms and the ants to finish it off before they could forget it had ever been there.

In the fields, cows formed little burial mounds, oval and white. Their bellies, full of gas, had inflated like balloons, then shriveled. They looked obese—obese and sleeping. As if these were fields of pale, giant molehills. Their legs held out straight from rigor mortis.

Corentin could not help but gaze at these corpses that were not human. It was terrible and fascinating. Something terrible and fascinating, about death.

Initially.

After a few fields, it was the same as with humans: he got used to it. His heart hardened, his eyes glazed over. He didn't stop anymore. They were dead, those cows, there was nothing to be done, you couldn't even eat them.

* * *

That evening, a moth burned in the fire Corentin had lit. Corentin was grief-stricken on seeing that insect, which had survived the catastrophe, die now in such a stupid way. It was absurd. Everything had been blown away, everything had been killed. Anything still alive—humans, animals, plants—was a miraculous survivor. A treasure. Such a precious thing, worth its weight in gold, even if gold wasn't worth anything anymore. Priceless creatures all, because with them the world could begin again.

And this thing came and burned its wings in the fire. It made a tiny hiss when it caught—then it fell, already ash, into the embers.

It was more than consternation: Corentin was angry.

It was as if Hercules, having completed his labors, died of a cold. As if God created the world then had a heart attack.

Ridiculous.

He looked at Blind Boy.

What could they do, the two of them.

What could they save, what could they restore to life.

And yet: they had to.

In that moment, when the moth went up in flames, he understood that it was their duty, to bring back life. They also had the power to continue, to resurrect. They were becoming gods.

Corentin stared at the puppy for a moment longer.

But how.

He shook his head.

They had to find the others. The only way was with others.

Basically, all alone they were useless. They might as well die.

They were poor, wretched little gods.

It gave him nightmares.

In the middle of a day Corentin would record as August 11, they entered the territory of the Forests. And in all likelihood, he would not have recognized them had he not remembered the shape of the roads and the curves of each bend, had he not been looking out for the illegible signposts and the farms he'd gone past a thousand times, had he not felt his body quiver with a new sense of proximity. Because there were no more Forests. And even though he'd expected this, it was a shock. He'd hoped for something else. He'd believed the Forests would be stronger, that there would be a magnificent surprise in store for him, that there was truly something magical about them. And now all that was nothing but legends. Their trees were like all the trees he had seen since leaving the Big City: bare, blackened, bent, or gashed open. Their rivers were gray and muddy, full of dead fish in a sluggish current. No birds sang. It was cold and clammy.

Like elsewhere. Like everywhere.

Something sank inside Corentin, shrinking him, when all he had hoped for was to be able to expand, to spread out at last after days of distress—he felt the flesh tightening around his bones.

He'd been searching for a sign, but all he found was indifference.

Deep in his gut, the feeling he'd been betrayed.

* * *

He went through the Forests without making a sound. The leaves did not crunch beneath his feet, they had fallen as ash. Pebbles did not roll. Incinerated by the fire of the world, they crumbled when Corentin stepped on them. Nothing announced its presence, neither squirrel nor blackbird, not even a fly, which, before, would have buzzed around him, driving him mad. A dozen times he thought he saw a blade of grass or a patch of tree that had been spared, that had preserved its colors, its green-brown bronze.

For something to gleam like bronze, it needed sunshine.

Corentin had slowed his pace, without realizing.

A part of him didn't want to get there. As long as he was still on the way, he had a goal. Hope, too, a hope which he tried to quell, not to be disappointed, but which slipped into his head like leaking water, through the tiniest gap, the slightest breach. He frequently blocked his ears, as if it were coming from outside. But it clung on, inside him. No, he said, no. He shook his arms, his shoulders, to make it fall. But the hope was still there, all the same.

Because he would get there eventually.

And Corentin could have gone on by, could have skipped the little turn-off. Could have gone on down the road indefinitely. Then there wouldn't have been any bitterness, any sorrow. He would never have known what had happened, down there.

But there wouldn't be any more goal, either. No more quest, nothing more to expect. He would go on—where? What for?

Simply go on.

It didn't make any sense.

In any case, whether he got there or didn't get there. In any case, the goal would come to an end.

And he reckoned that his legs couldn't go any further. He reckoned they needed to rest. And then: he'd see, afterwards.

If there was anyone left alive in the Forests—down there, he'd have his answer.

He caught his breath.

In the last little valley, where the road wound down, a sinuous trail, and there was nothing more after the two bends—in the last little valley, he began humming, very softly, to give himself courage.

* * *

And what he found at last: at the end of the valley, in the hole where he'd grown up, there was the house.

And in the house, there was Augustine.

But as soon as he saw her, he wasn't sure anymore. Was it really Augustine?

Something was moving and breathing.

It was making a little noise.

Corentin went in after knocking gently.

He'd seen her, but he called out all the same.

Augustine.

She didn't turn her head toward him. She was in the armchair, her hands placed flat on her thighs, on the old apron she wore all day long. It reminded him of the old couple he'd left by the wood stove. They were stiff like that, too, just as motionless.

He walked into the room, knelt down to be level with her.

Augustine.

Maybe she saw him. He thought he saw a fleeting shadow cross her face.

He had never been a shadow.

Or else, this was the only thing left and he'd have to make do with it, but just then, he didn't understand. He held out his hand to her, very slowly, very gently. When he touched her, she didn't recoil. She didn't tremble. She didn't do anything.

Oh the sudden doubt, so strong Corentin almost faltered.

He touched her shoulder.

Was she really alive?

If he pushed her, would she fall to one side, because she'd been dead for days, as if she'd been waiting for him, wedged in the armchair opposite the door to be sure to see him if he came?

Since he never came.

I'm here, he said.

His voice catching.

He shoved her, gently.

She didn't fall.

C orentin.

He turned around, slowly, hearing her call to him. He didn't recognize her at first, her face, her figure— but her voice.

Of course he knew.

He'd promised himself not to look at her anymore, not to speak to her. Something inside him, too young and too fragile—something had never gotten over her rejection. She had sworn to be a recluse, lost behind the thick walls of a cold abbey. Life had gotten the better of her childhood convictions. She'd forgotten. She'd married young. They both worked the land. Two years earlier, she'd had a son.

She was just a liar. Corentin didn't want to say her name.

But that was before.

Since then, there'd been the thing, everything was dead.

And she was there.

Standing in the door.

Blind Boy was on his hind legs licking her fingers. She gave a pale smile. So Corentin blinked, his head spun briefly. It came out in a breath.

Mathilde.

Just then, Augustine opened her eyes wide, it was as if she suddenly realized he was there—had she been thinking, until now, that he was Mathilde? Could she still see with those faded irises of hers that were the color of the gray sky?

She stifled a cry and held out her fleshless arms to him.

* * *

The two women were the only ones left. Two sole survivors in the Forests, Mathilde and Augustine—Augustine with her hand firmly held, Corentin would not let her go.

Augustine who was trembling.

Who managed a few words, her voice softer than a murmur.

What happened here? asked Corentin in one breath.

The old lady said, I saw it.

Oh, not much. Just a tiny fraction of an instant of the catastrophe, maybe the moment when it all started. When everything had been carried away, when the fire went over—she couldn't find any other words. If she'd seen more, if she'd found the words, she would be dead.

She had just reached for the handle of the door leading from the cellar, and something held her back. She'd gone back to the far end to put away some boxes. She didn't know what had happened. She'd felt this dull, terrifying earthquake, and in a sort of strangely instinctive gesture, she'd hurried to close the door to the cellar behind her. And it was there through the cracked-open door that she saw the beginning of the thing. Not saw: glimpsed. Not even: suddenly she lost consciousness.

She didn't know when she had to come to.

She didn't know when she went outside.

She didn't want to speak about the destructive force that had come.

Corentin acquiesced in silence. He squeezed her hand tighter.

Augustine was there. Their hearts were beating together— too fast.

He looked at Mathilde.

What about you.

And she looked down and wiped her tears.

We mustn't speak about it.

Corentin nodded. He wouldn't ask again. He took her hand, too, but she pulled it away.

* * *

He slept in the attic with Blind Boy, climbing up the outside stairway that led to the old wooden door, loose on its hinges. Mathilde had a bed downstairs next to Augustine's. All night long, she added more wood to the fire. Old people die from the cold, she said. He could hear the dull sound of the logs dropping into the hearth—he had brought his mattress closer to the chimney shaft to make the most of the bit of warmth.

He felt disheartened. His return was nothing like what he'd hoped. There was no joy. Nor was there any great sorrow—neither happiness nor pain. Some diffuse sensation crawled through his veins, a latent sadness, a feeling that should have been cheerful but just couldn't be.

There. He'd made it.

The road had come to an end—and now?

Fear.

He closed his eyes, squeezing so tight it hurt. It stung, beneath his lids.

Now what do we do?

We live. We survive.

But why? How long? How?

The very questions they'd been asking in the catacombs, not three weeks ago. They'd been laughing. Their answers were complete nonsense. Now he had to find answers, urgently.

Now what do we do?

Maybe that was it, the pain in his gut.

And why—to die a little later, a little lonelier.

His thoughts were all knotted up inside him. A huge white veil covered them, and they led nowhere. The direction was missing. Not left or right: the direction that makes you get up in the morning. Whenever he tried to make sense of it all, Corentin put his head in his hands and squeezed so hard his bones cracked.

What to do, what to do. Everything that only yesterday you took for granted.

His strength had vanished.

He'd believed he would save Augustine—but Augustine hadn't needed him in order to survive or to begin dying.

On his own, there was nothing he wanted. It was for her. For someone else. On his own—nothing interested him, he might as well die right now.

He'd never wondered what might happen when he got to the Forests.

Not "when."

Just after.

He'd always said, We'll see.

Well, now he saw. He'd got here at the end of his journey and now he had seen for himself what he hadn't wanted to accept before: there was nothing left here either. And this time, he wasn't referring to the burned, deserted world, the ashes up to his eyebrows. He was talking about hope, future, desire. It was to this that the answer was *nothing*.

* * *

Don't move. Don't expand.
Live like a worm.
Never see the day again.

It was raining outside.
The hydrangea had been in bloom but—
It stayed dark inside.
There was some wind.
The only gesture, the only movement of the earth.
In fact, everything is dead, he thought.

And yet he got up.

At what a price, he would think, later.

It was like being uprooted all over again, like on the first day after he left the catacombs: an unknown suffering, the sense he was severing every tie that held him to the ground and that was part of him—like an absolute urge to cut his own flesh into strips he could bury, so as not to face the world because it was too trying, and he was sinking into the mud with them, he had to pull himself out, tear himself away, his heart was pounding, his body covered in sweat.

He got to his feet, and that changed so little.

For days he'd held out, to get this far, and now his legs would hardly carry him. He'd found the strength, he'd taken everything, demanded everything, and he had nothing left inside that would keep him going—and anyway, there was no reason anymore to keep going.

He looked at himself in a little mirror hanging on the wall by the single window. He'd lost weight. He'd gone gray—his skin, his eyes, his hair, as if something had been extinguished, something that had bogged down his entire being. His beard had grown a little. He ran his hand over it, and through his dark hair that he had not managed to untangle, matted as it was with sweat and ash. When his fingers scratched at his face, they left a lighter trace and the dirt collected under his nails.

Suddenly he could not stand himself. He was disgusting.

He did not recognize the young man in the reflection. He saw someone, and for a moment he wondered who it was.

Because *this* could not be him.

Not somebody.

This thing.

So, going up to the mirror, he understood that the world would have won if he became the animal he saw in the reflection. If he stuck to eating straight out of the pan, reheating at random whatever gruel he found among the cans, dipping his hands into it then wiping them on his sleeves, and when his sleeves became revolting, on his trouser legs, already splattered with stains; he ignored the fact that now there were Mathilde and Augustine, and that he owed them some sort of restraint, of the sort that would keep him from scratching himself like some beast simply because it itched, or from opening his fly to piss whenever he felt like it, and wherever, or from no longer washing, from stinking and not giving a damn, from rolling in the mud with Blind Boy simply because there was nothing else to do.

He would become less than a man if he stopped talking, if he stopped hoping, if he stopped setting himself a tiny goal every day; if he closed the door to the attic and simply waited for Mathilde to bring him some food while he just stayed there lying on the old floor—eating, sleeping, moaning, starting all over again the next day, and the day after that, and every day that followed.

And that wouldn't do.

* * *

That was why he forced himself to get up, even though he was worn out, even though his very skin ached and wanted to stay on the floor—that was how he saw himself, like a pig wallowing in the mire dreaming of only one thing, never to move again, its back in the shit and its belly offered to the sun and the butcher's knife, and one day it would be killed, that was all it was good for, to feed something else, and even then—it would smell of silt, and peat, and ruin, it would smell of evil and no one would want to eat it.

On your feet.

He took the mirror off the wall, put it on the floor face down so it would not reflect anything anymore.

Don't want to see that.

He needed strength.

He needed courage.

Even to go down the stairs and adjust his face the moment he went into the warm room where Mathilde and Augustine would turn their heads to him.

It was so stupid but: he was a man.

He was the one who—was going to help them, was going to save them.

It wasn't in his head: it was in his genes, in every molecule in his body, in the stench from his exhausted brain.

Man.

How he wished he could make himself tiny—so small he could fit in a hand, and be stroked and cherished, become Blind Boy, who he carried on his back and fed and picked up when the puppy couldn't cope—and what about him, who had carried him, who had picked him up, who would help him when it got too hard?

He was a man and he would have to play that role until his dying day: that is what filled up all the space in his head.

He leaned against the doorframe.

Don't want to.

He would be the one who supported others, and whom no one else ever supported. The one who held out his hand—not the one who reached for another's. The one who enveloped, reassured, faced up, even though he was dying of fear and cold and fatigue, the one others counted on, and who counted the hours until evening, and the days until death, when it would be time to stop, when there would be rest, at last, and he could forget that he had to lie and be strong and tall and tireless.

He would be all of that—just had to take it in, and get used to it.

He would, he had come back for that.

He would find his momentum.

He would overcome his conviction that no amount of reasoning or urgency could surmount the unbelievable weakness that had him in its grip.

Corentin stood up—but it took him all this time.

Every new moment of awareness hurt; he tried to crush them, one after the other. To live in this world required unconsciousness, required madness. He thrust his face into his hands, hunting through the darkness and oblivion.

It could have gone on like that for years.

But he was on his feet.

It could have gone on for years, but it didn't.

It was faster than that.

It was terrible.

Because there was a cry.

Not a cry: a scream.

Human—scarcely.

But what else could it be besides human.

Then Corentin leapt up, grabbed the rifle, and scrambled down the staircase.

Mathilde was standing stock still in the middle of the room, paralyzed, her fists clenched against her body. She was looking into the distance—deep inside. Her lips were trembling, her hands were red with blood. There was blood all the way to the floor. The tiles shining scarlet.

Corentin's voice caught in his throat. Then he shouted her name. Not Mathilde: Augustine, he couldn't see her.

No, no, what have you done.

He ran into the kitchen.

Augustine was there, he nearly knocked her over. She was walking toward him, taking tiny steps, wheezing and holding a big basin half-filled with water. He took it from her.

Augustine.

I saw it.

There was her voice, suddenly. Rasping, aged, fearful—her voice had come back. He recognized it. Augustine was alive. Corentin's heart suddenly began to beat again, palpitations unleashed by fear, the fear that perhaps Mathilde—Mathilde who had lost everything, and whose mind seemed to falter at times—Augustine was alive.

But Corentin didn't get it at first, didn't realize—would realize later on. In his panic, he was still touching the old woman, looking for a wound.

Augustine, the blood.

I saw it.

She waved him away.

* * *

This too, the thing had killed.

Mathilde didn't know, before.

No one knew.

The thing itself had taken some time, because the embryo was well hidden. But the thing had eventually gotten the better of her, and from deep inside Mathilde's belly, the embryo had let go.

So much blood, Corentin would think, afterwards.

He would stand there just before the screens Augustine had put up in the room downstairs for some privacy. He wouldn't dare go beyond them. He would call out in a quiet voice and not once did Mathilde reply.

He would knock, timidly, four light little taps on the delicate wood, not to wake her if she was asleep.

She slept all the time. Or pretended to. In any case, she didn't respond, didn't show her face. Only Augustine could *go in*.

Please.

Mathilde didn't hear.

Augustine went by, her expression grave. She pushed Corentin out of the way.

This is no place for a man.

Man.

Like a curse.

He closed his eyes.

He spent his time curled up by the wood stove, listening out for a sound, a voice. At night, in the attic, with his ear close to the chimney shaft, he waited for a sign that didn't come.

They had their assigned roles, of necessity. Corentin helped, prepared, tidied, brought in wood. Mathilde stayed curled up under the blanket, begged them to darken the room for her. Then stopped begging. Who knows what was still there under the comforter—a ghost, denial, hurt.

Corentin couldn't help but stare, whenever he went by, at the shapeless mound under the sheets.

How could she breathe under there.

He went by and he looked at Mathilde, buried, and it made him think of the white cow corpses he had seen on his way, she looked like a dromedary's hump, or a huge bump, or an animal swallowed by a boa constrictor, or a bed with sheets rumpled in a violent haste.

She looked like a woman who had no child anymore, at all.

Silence filled the house.

* * *

One morning, it was the fourth day, Mathilde got up. She came upon Corentin in the kitchen. The violet shadows beneath her eyes seemed to devour her face; her eyes were red with sorrow. There were lines along her cheeks and down the sides of her face, and Corentin hoped they were marks left by the pillow, but they weren't, they really were lines of fatigue and suffering. She looked away.

Don't say anything.

He took her hand.

She yanked it away.

And so they acted as if everything was normal.

* * *

For a long time, Alice had kept a donkey, and now at her place Corentin found a cart. So one morning he left for the Little Town to help himself to all the supplies he could find.

Mathilde's scream had been like the lash of a whip. He

couldn't give up. He couldn't go on saying he was unhappier than anyone, or that he had no more strength. So what else could he do now, other than join in the insane circle dance of ephemeral survival.

Augustine was extremely thin. Was it since, or had she always—he couldn't remember. She organized. She planned. She took care of. She tired quickly. Mathilde, white as a ghost: she made Augustine sit in the armchair several times a day.

Augustine had taken a walk around the garden. She came back shrugging her shoulders.

There's nothing left, Corentin whispered, with the ridiculous hope that she might contradict him.

Well now, she said.

And that was all.

Well now, Corentin would echo defiantly, looking outside, harnessing the cart, stopping mid-climb to catch his breath.

He'd stuffed the little cart with everything he found, lashed it all together with ropes so it wouldn't spill out. He would go back to the Little Town many times: twenty-three, to be exact. Every trip would take an entire gray day. Corentin's arms became stalks of pain, his legs, raw bones. His breathing too hoarse in his chest. He would go on. It was their life which he was stockpiling in the Little Town, which he brought back on those days of fatigue.

The thing had gone through there on market day. Corentin wandered around the marketplace among the scorched stalls, the burned goods, the burned figures. There was nothing left.

And he wondered how many times since the catastrophe he had said: there's nothing left.

Nothing.

This word would have sufficed to speak of the world from then on.

He wandered for a long time. Maybe he was expecting to come upon some living souls, even if he didn't believe he would—the shops seemed intact. The shelves of merchandise had not been looted, the products had not been moved. Eight thousand people in one blow.

Eight thousand, and nobody.

T here was never a sound, ever, along the road between the Forests and the Little Town.

His ears buzzed. But the buzzing wasn't outside, it was inside Corentin's head. A reaction to the extreme muteness of the world. A rustling inside to make him believe there was something.

How to fill that void.

Corentin couldn't sing all the time. He couldn't talk to the dog—he didn't know what to say to him.

And all the way back to the Forests he thought about Augustine and Mathilde.

Where the silence was broken, fitfully.

A tiny victory.

The supplies lined up in the pantry, too.

He didn't think about anything, basically. Nothing at all yet.

* * *

Mathilde—as if there had never been that scream, or the blood, or the tears. Life had reclaimed Mathilde. She was a bit slower, a bit sadder. One evening she said:

Something died for the second time.

She knew it didn't exist.

But it was what she felt in her guts.

Not a void: a hollow.

More than a void. It went farther, gaped wider. Something staggering.

Corentin and even Augustine: they didn't understand. They couldn't. It was not their belly that had been sucked out. Not their guts, which she thought had left her body, it hurt so much.

Yes, it hurt.

In her heart.

She buried it, hidden like treasure. Her sorrow. It wouldn't heal. It belonged to her.

Her life.

It went on, there was nothing to be done.

* * *

At the top of the gutted little road, Corentin put up a wooden sign. He had written: WE ARE HERE.

Because no one would think to go looking deep in the valley. A living person might go by without seeing them, without suspecting. Even the smoke from the chimney, on a misty day, was imperceptible.

We are here.

Why say it.

Who would come this far. The road didn't lead anywhere, only to another devastated village, to black fallow fields. It went deeper into the countryside. It offered no escape.

If there were any living people left, they wouldn't come as far as the Forests. They would flee.

But where.

There were no more migrating birds to show the way. Corentin didn't know where to go, where the world might have been a bit less destroyed, where some niches might remain, precarious shelters, sources of translucent water.

To stay.

What madness.

It was too early to think differently. The shock was still

resonating, paralyzing minds and bodies. And yet, Corentin felt, to the depths of his soul, that he must go away.

But it was impossible.

He didn't know anywhere else.

Augustine wouldn't have the strength to get anywhere else.

Nor would he.

For the moment, he was walking six hours a day to fill the cart and bring back supplies, blankets, clothing—it was like the old woman who had taken him in on the road a few days ago had said: everything, even things that seem useless. The house wasn't big enough. He had stored most of his finds in the barn.

WE ARE HERE.

Maybe, if others came, he would find the impetus to follow them and leave the Forests behind, forever.

In the meantime, he didn't budge.

No one budged.

The days went by terrifyingly slowly. When it rained, Corentin stayed by the fire, his gaze fading from staring so long at the rain streaming down the bits of wood and plastic he had nailed over the broken window panes.

In another time, he could have been working the earth in the garden, getting it ready for winter, then for spring. He could have been picking mushrooms, chestnuts, walnuts.

That didn't exist anymore.

He could go out and walk in the rain. He knew there would be no mushrooms, no chestnuts, no walnuts. He could work the earth: there were no more seeds to plant.

In another time: a month and a half ago.

But now.

And it hadn't been there right after the catastrophe. It hadn't been there when he was in shock with his wild joy at having survived. Or during the journey, as long as he went on hoping. It was there now, since his return: the immense, horrible void.

Now that Corentin was here. Now that he'd found Augustine and Mathilde. Now that—he didn't know what to do anymore.

Of course, he wasn't alone now: but all three of them were alone. An unbearable wilderness all around them. The silence, enough to make you scream at night to make it stop at last. His mind, more than anything, thinking when he didn't want it to, wailing that they would die here, in this hole, that the Reaper would come for them one by one and in spite of the fear, there would be this strange relief, no more wondering why they had to put up with a pointless tomorrow, and then another. But until then, years would go by. Maybe dozens of years.

And every day of every year, there would be nothing.

No goal, no expectation, no desire. No hope.

Sitting by the fire. Standing in the rain.

Standing by the fire. Sitting in the rain.

Like an animal in a cage that would rather die, except that—

There was instinct. Survival. Preservation. And no matter what Corentin said, that fucking hope that wouldn't give up.

But they were alone, and that was no good.

You can't remake the world when there are only three of you.

* * *

The words were dancing in his head—the great extinction. He'd often heard people speak about it, before. When some of them had tried to sound the alarm. They gave numbers, they gave examples. How in the summer, when you drove somewhere, there were no more bugs squashed on the windshield of your car. That was how it began, extinction.

The sixth.

The previous one had seen the disappearance of the dinosaurs. Sixty-five million years ago. Why was it happening again in this infinitesimal period of time when he, Corentin, was on earth, why, during these microscopic eighty years that were supposed to make up his existence, had this new extinction come—but hadn't it been like this right from the start, the rotten luck, the jinx, the curse, wasn't it obvious, actually, that the world would come to an end just then.

The Holocene. The word filled him with fear. It began like *holocaust*. It was idiotic and petrifying.

When three quarters of all living species disappear, for whatever reason—a meteor, volcanoes gone mad, climate change, human activity. Not even activity: presence. The moment humans arrived on the planet, the living creatures in their midst began to go extinct.

Already in pre-historical times.

Too much hunting. Too much blood.

Intrinsically, human beings were murderers. They stank of death. As stupid as those cancer cells destroying the body that hosts them, until finally they die from it. Kill and be killed.

Insane.

Corentin looked at the gray-black landscapes. He didn't doubt it. He said it in a hushed voice, to get used to the idea.

Extinction.

And the words that ought to be on the little sign at the top of the valley weren't, WE ARE HERE.

They were, HERE WE ARE.

Augustine had been mending an old dishcloth for weeks. When she finished, she cried out.

Oh damn. Damn.

She unpicked the thread and started over. There was only one dishcloth to repair. She must have mended it thirty times.

Mathilde tidied.

But there was nothing left to tidy, so she sat outside and stared into space for hours.

What are you looking at, said Corentin.

She shrugged.

Television.

He leveled his gaze at her back, but she didn't turn around. He frowned, unsure whether she was making fun of him, or going mad.

She let out a sigh, with a faint smile she sometimes had.

Nothing. I'm not looking at anything, I'm pretending.

Don't you want to come in. It's cold.

She shook her head.

The program isn't over yet.

* * *

He got in the habit of taking Blind Boy for a walk. If he stayed in the house, he went around in circles, grumbled, sighed and leaned against the walls that were barely lukewarm.

The puppy had grown, his paws had gotten considerably

wider, as if they were waiting for the rest to follow. Corentin wondered how big he'd be when fully grown. Whether he was normal. Whether he would become a monster, because of the catastrophe, which had disrupted everything. He kept an eye on him. The dog looked like a baby that has grown up all of a sudden, running through the icy rain.

After the strange back-and-forth between hot and cold, the temperatures had dropped for good. Corentin buttoned his jacket up to the collar. He remembered the warnings they'd heard for years, that the earth was heating too much and too quickly—and it was true: so many marine species had already disappeared from the oceans, which had become abnormally warm and acidic; so many mammals, too, in regions overcome by desertification, which made them uninhabitable. Animals had been the first to suffer from the changes in the world, and not one human being had ever thought that they might be next. Or there had been so few of them. So often they'd been silenced. The heat had risen in insidious little increments—painless, invisible—until there was nothing left to be done, because everything had already been set in motion, there was no going back, no matter how you wept and begged, this was the grand machinery of the universe.

But once everything had imploded, when the stifling heat had burned the world, the opposite happened. The heat faded away, the sun disappeared. Was it the ash which had caused this sort of impact winter—but there had been no impact, at least as far as Corentin could tell, but he didn't actually know. And the question went on haunting him, even though there was no answer: not knowing was a sort of protection, almost a reassurance. But also—an immense fear, because it could come back, and he couldn't tell if it was coming, couldn't recognize it. So he had to stop asking himself that question. It had come. It was over. And now only everyday survival, one day at a time, was what counted. It was cold, and that was that.

Corentin thought: extinction. He thought: glaciation.

But he had to stop thinking so he went out with the dog.

He went for a long time.

He went, period.

He looked at the Forests and they reminded him of an India ink drawing, they reminded him of skeletons someone might have painted in black with the regularity and fierce determination of a sick person. He felt tiny beneath the awning of tall trees. In fact, it was no longer an awning, just a space of naked trunks and long empty branches that sometimes broke off for no reason. Corentin could hear them cracking, and he would look up to get out of the way, quickly, the branches were falling, it was deadwood, they crumbled as they crashed to the ground. He would pick up pieces, afterwards, and set them next to the wood stove when he got home.

It was sort of like winter: the Forests had no more leaves, no more colors. They got your feet wet, and your back and shoulders, too, when it rained, and the rain dripped down along the branches stripped of their bark. Like some lunar earth. There was nothing left. Corentin could see far beyond the labyrinth of trees: there was no vegetation to block the horizon. But what was the point, since there was nothing left to see, either—he searched through the small valleys with Blind Boy, looking for the slightest sign of life—a mushroom, a leaf, an insect.

Gradually, all the paths were erased by the accumulation of dead wood, and to go walking meant taking long strides, climbing over, going around. Everything was dry and burned. Everything was gray and yellow and brown. Sometimes Corentin would stop in front of a charred bramble bush and touch its thorns: they fell. When he reached the top of a hill he looked out at the landscape and tried not to tremble. The world was a vastness of dust.

It was sort of like winter and Corentin tried to get used to it: it would last for years. He would go home again slowly, his eyes glued to his shoes not to see the ugliness and bleakness all around him. At other times he would look at the Forests, and he forced his imagination to color them again. It's a drawing, he said to himself. In his mind there were colored pencils and felt tips and gouache paints. He smeared green on the trees and blue in the river beds, and palettes of yellow and pale orange in the ripening meadows. He added dots of red for wild strawberries, and pink for digitalis; he distilled white acacia trees, could smell their delicious scent, recalled the fritters Augustine used to make when he was a child. For a few seconds, a few minutes, he re-created color, he remade the world. It was not with strokes of genius but with the strokes of a brush, of memories and hope. He swept the image up in his arms, as if he could hold it still. He wanted to tell Mathilde and Augustine, he wanted to show them. But by the time he got home, it had all evaporated.

Blind Boy ferreted among the trees, sniffing them, pissing on half of them. No one will fight him for this territory, thought Corentin. No one would want any of this.

And in any case, there was no one anymore.

Or so he thought.

It was while he was on one of these walks that he met some survivors. There were four of them. Men. They were hungry.

Corentin didn't like their expression when they asked for something to eat. He didn't like the way they came toward him, abreast, from behind the trees, their faces tense, their gazes malevolent. Blind Boy growled quietly next to him; he didn't like them either.

Corentin forced himself to answer them without recoiling. He was emanating something, and he hoped it was invisible; a shiver, a rancid smell, a sourness he immediately recognized— it was fear. He knew he had to make the men go away, send them along another path that wouldn't lead anywhere near the house, anywhere near Mathilde and Augustine.

He said:

There are supplies in the Little Town. If you go that way, you'll be there in two hours.

What about you.

I don't have anything.

Where have you come from.

I haven't come from anywhere.

Where are you going.

Nowhere.

He didn't have a pack. They wondered where his things were.

I don't have anything.

You can't survive if you don't have anything.

I'm not interested in surviving.

They didn't believe him. They came too close.

Don't touch me. What good will it do you.

Shut your fucking face, they said.

He raised his hands in a gesture of conciliation.

It's a two-hour walk to the town. Two hours is nothing.

You must have a place. A shelter. A cabin.

Corentin would never take them there. Never let those expressions—or those hands that began shoving and hitting him suddenly, furiously.

Blind Boy barked. They began beating him.

Stop. He's just a puppy.

They kept on. Blind Boy managed to escape, whimpering. Then they went for Corentin. Their hands were stiff and hard. They threw him on the ground and beat him as long as they had the strength, and Corentin felt that, more than anything, it was the world they had it in for, all the wretchedness and pain, the entire disgusting future, it wasn't really against him, he just happened to be there, rotten luck—they were bludgeoning him, breathlessly, to vent their anger, but it wasn't because of him, maybe he would have done the same if he was hungry and cold and afraid the way they were.

It's not me, it's not me.

They didn't stop.

They left him unconscious, lying in the mud. They took his coat and shoes and scarf.

As they left, they spat on him.

Fucking asshole.

* * *

Later, Blind Boy brought Mathilde to him.

Later, Corentin would think that if the men had still been

there when she arrived—no, he wouldn't go there, he didn't want to think about it.

Hush, hush.

It brought tears to his eyes.

He had headaches, and bruises, and ached all through his body for over a week.

If the men had still been there. He couldn't get the thought out of his mind. At night the faintest noise startled him.

There was no noise. His imagination was making them up, the creaking sounds and cries.

He took his rifle wherever he went.

As soon as he could, he took down the sign at the top of the valley.

The men never came back.

But it had started, he knew it.

The feral days.

It had caught Corentin unawares, because he hadn't thought it would be so soon. He'd thought that because there was still plenty of food, and so few survivors, there would be no war—and now the war had come.

They were crazy, said Mathilde.

They were men, he replied.

They'd lost their way.

There would be others.

* * *

The cold didn't let up. It was much too soon, but the seasons were all out of sync. Before, the heat would have forced them to find shelter.

Now it was the cold.

But why.

As if they even needed a reason. It was cold, dammit, it was really cold.

So, after he'd brought back all the piles of firewood from the hamlet to the barn, he gathered together the old axes and stared at them. He had never used an ax. He'd never seen anyone use an ax. He could only remember chainsaws, in the woods, the noise of their motors piercing his eardrums.

He looked at the tall dark forests.

What if winter lasted forever.

In any case, the trees were dead. He might as well chop them down. He started with the smallest ones that weren't more than twenty or twenty-five feet tall. Not as hard. Not as scary.

But really hard all the same. Enough to make you think that the thing, when it burned them, had turned them into steel. Enough for Corentin to conclude that he would never be able to strike them hard enough to make a dent, let alone chop and fell them. Every time the ax blade struck the trunk, the vibrations went all the way through his shoulders, up to his brain. He had terrible headaches. He didn't give up.

His hands bled in spite of the rags he rolled around them, he couldn't keep them closed anymore—his fists opened with every blow, the ax fell from his hands, he was wiping away sweat along with tears. His back had hardened into an old man's posture. In the evening when he came home and saw himself in the few windowpanes still intact, he was stunned.

Gradually, however, he accumulated and stacked piles of wood one next to the other. The first pile, because he didn't know how to stack it level, fell over on its side during the night; he stacked it again the next morning, weeping with rage. Everything took hours.

How much time would it take, if he had a chainsaw.

But time was something he had stacks and stacks of.

The problem was strength.

What would it be like when they started to run out of

food—so he had to make the most of it, had to strike and chop, years in advance, for the days of weakness. On he went. He wouldn't stop until he lined up seventy cords in the yard.

For the first time he had to admit that *this*—the state of the world, the absence of everything, the end that just never seemed to end—might last for years.

In the evening, once he'd finally managed to stretch out full length on his mattress, close up against the chimney shaft for warmth, he couldn't sleep. He was in too much pain. He tried to find a comfortable position. He waited for exhaustion. For sleep, at last.

At dawn—none of them knew what time it was—the first sound came from downstairs. He could hear it through the chimney, the sound of dishes, Mathilde getting the cups out for the coffee, with sugar while it lasted.

With his hands flat on the faint warmth of the brick, he kept his eyes closed.

Sooner or later, he would find the energy to get up. He would find the energy to go down the stairs, to eat, and set off to the woods.

But not right away.

The blood had to start circulating again, his strength had to return.

He had to roll over to the edge of the bed and wait patiently for the pins and needles to stop, the ones that made electric shocks in his elbows and feet and fingertips; until his joints stopped cracking with every movement, even the tiniest, so that he could stand up without collapsing, the way he had one morning, a few days earlier—when he'd finally made it downstairs, Mathilde asked him about the noise; he said he'd dropped his pack.

He had to go about it slowly. He began by moving his fingers. It felt as if they were falling off, one after the other. He soaked them in the basin of water next to him to rinse off the blood and pus from the little sores that weren't healing. His skin pulled as if it were too tight.

His body loosened, muscle by muscle, nerve by nerve. It was like opening some piece of rusty machinery, trying not to break it. Corentin was sure that one morning, he'd find his bones piercing his flesh. He hadn't been prepared for this. He had never thought that, one day, his existence would be reduced to this exhaustion and pain radiating all through his flesh.

But he had no choice. He had to start again, over and over.

He didn't protest. He didn't try to avoid it.

It was just this staggering realization.

So this was life.

M athilde was helping him stack wood. She had blue eyes, red cheeks. There was sweat on her brow, and she hooked her coat over a stray picket.

Don't do that, said Corentin. You'll get cold.

I'll put it right back on.

Don't do it.

You're only wearing a shirt.

It's not the same thing.

There were no curves under his shirt.

Mathilde had seen the way Corentin looked at her.

She'd seen it, but it had no effect on her—neither pleasure, nor desire, nor fear. It had slipped over her, like always, she hadn't noticed any difference.

She was used to him the way she was used to the dog. She never saw him, not really. Of course, sometimes their eyes met, but she didn't attach herself to him, she didn't *enter* him. She barely grazed him, and her thoughts immediately fluttered away to the tree behind her, or the rock crumbling below the dead broom bushes, or the dried branches she snapped over her knee and took inside for kindling.

She answered his questions without thinking or looking up, she avoided him when he was in the room the way she avoided a wall. Not paying any attention. Instinctively. To Mathilde, Corentin was part of the furniture. He was the only one left; she made do with his presence, no moods, no anger.

At dinner she served him after Augustine.

She didn't say good morning or good night, nothing when he came down from the attic in the morning, nothing when he went back up with a weary step after nightfall. She began her sentences with no introduction—time to bring in some wood, Augustine's tired this morning, the coffee's ready.

She didn't smile a lot. She had her reasons, she thought, when she realized she was sad—she had lost everything.

And he was just there, that was all.

Corentin or anyone else.

Corentin or the dog.

That was her impression on the rare occasions when she wondered. The only thing that existed was their survival. It took all their strength, all their planning.

Mathilde saw the way Corentin looked at her, but what was in that look did not reach her. She did not realize what she was at that moment, in her shirtsleeves in the chill air of the world: warm, living flesh.

A terrible temptation.

* * *

After he reached his seventy cords, Corentin went on chopping wood. There was nothing else to do. Sometimes he would think that everything had bloomed again during the night, and he'd open his eyes in the morning, convinced he would see the sun and colors. The leaden landscape made him sigh.

All the ugliness of the world.

He worked in the rain—he'd had to resign himself to it, it had been raining for seventeen days.

A cold rain. That too was something he had to face, he had to forget the hope of almost-warm afternoons.

Twice a day, at noon and in the evening, he would dry his muddy, soaking clothes by the fire. When it was time to put them back on, they were still stiff and damp. It felt as if he were sliding into long icy pockets. So yes, they gave him the courage to go back to striking trees, to keep warm somehow until it was time to change into dry trousers and sweater at the end of the day, before a meal that was not very filling, because Mathilde was saving on supplies—he dreamt of a huge steak and roast potatoes—then nighttime in his little room, which was cold, too, despite the chimney shaft.

The rain was still acidic. He had rashes on his skin here and there, wherever drops of water could get in easily—on his neck, his face, his hands. He'd gotten used to it. He would rub olive oil on his skin to calm the burning sensation. Water had become a danger.

Down at the end of the valley, the stream was lively now and murmured in little black eddies, rushing against its banks, splashing as it went by; but there didn't seem to be anything living in its flow—no fish, or insects, or crawfish. He checked it every morning. Because sooner or later they'd have no bottled water left and this water had to be crystal-clear again, they'd have to drink it, even if it meant boiling it first. He wouldn't risk it until he saw some creatures living there first. For the moment, there was nothing and no one in the water or at the edge, nowhere. So he turned his back on the stream and went back up to the house past the gray woods.

The gray sky, too.

Maybe a bit less so—perhaps it was just an impression.

But all the same.

As if this never-ending drizzle were making the dust fall, cleansing the air. The day before, in spite of the rain, Corentin could just make out the disc of the sun behind the cloudbanks. There was a terrifying black dot right in the middle.

* * *

Life was unspeakably sad, and Augustine was finding it difficult to keep up with it. Everything about her had slowed
down. Whether it was the lack of light, their existence that had
become so hard, or simply age—she hardly spoke anymore,
she measured out her gestures, enough to make you think she
was counting her steps, counting her words, counting the
hours that just didn't seem to go by for her, either.

Withdrawn into herself. Hunched over. Corentin thought
that, protected in this way, she would live to a hundred.

She said as much in her croaking voice.

I'll be one hundred years old soon.

Mathilde qualified her words. You've still got a way to go
before you turn a hundred.

One hundred years—that's too long. Too long for a human
being.

They argued.

So many people who died when all they wanted was to live,
and here she was, this old woman, complaining.

Corentin got involved in the end, placing a hand on his
great-grandmother's quivering arm.

There are only three of us in this world and here you are
squabbling like fishwives.

The old woman lowered her gaze and he smiled at her, and
reassured her.

We need you.

I'm no good for anything anymore. Just another useless
mouth to feed.

We need you. You'll see.

A faint little spark in her old eyes.

You think so.

You'll see.

There were no more stars at night.

Well, there must have been, because the universe had not been destroyed. It was life that had been annihilated, but the earth was still turning, and the sun was still shining, even behind the clouds and ash and soot, and the stars still existed.

They couldn't see them anymore, was all.

But it was just as if.

As if there were no more stars.

And anyway, you could no longer lose yourself staring at the sky, there was nothing left to dream about.

That was all.

* * *

Mathilde was still sleeping next to Augustine.

She was keeping her from dying, Corentin thought.

And yet.

There were no more doctors, no more hospitals. How could you manage without doctors or hospitals, how could you manage when you didn't know what to do.

Augustine was tired, she was losing her appetite.

No tests were possible. No x-ray, scan, blood test. Corentin looked at the dozens of boxes of medication he'd brought from the town and piled up in a large cabinet, and they were all useless. What was needed was a doctor and a hospital. And they had all burned.

His helplessness was driving him crazy.

He hadn't lied. He needed Augustine. Like a child who thinks he's grown up and suddenly understands that he hasn't learned to live on his own yet—a person whose greatest terror is being abandoned, because absence is desertion.

He couldn't imagine the house without Augustine. He wanted her to live forever.

Please, he begged, looking at her.

She could hardly hear. She didn't hear.

All three of them were tired. All three of them had the same bleary complexion and the lack of strength of people who live without light, since the sun was still hidden behind that strange low-lying sky. And how can the world begin again, Corentin thought, if there's no more sun and no more warmth.

His walks with Blind Boy had turned into a desperate quest. He took a long stick and methodically searched the earth for some sign of life. He was sure it would begin in the soil, in a place where something—buried deep, protected, taking months or years to reemerge—might have survived; it would reemerge, he could feel it, willed it. It would make its way through the ash, and once again there would be plants, and once again nature would grow, and the spring water would return: they'd be able to feed themselves.

There were times, during these long rambles, when Corentin was no longer lucid; his vision flickering in his eyes as they scanned every inch of space and everything blurred; he frowned, continued on his way, rubbed his face. He only got up in the morning because of this expectancy: that nature would take the upper hand again.

He could not resign himself to the idea that nature might already have taken the upper hand by destroying everything. There had to be an afterwards. There was a future.

And in this future, the power of the earth triumphed over the void.

In this future, something would be reborn.
In this future, Augustine would die.

At other times, a thought occurred to Corentin, insidiously.
A filthy, despicable little thought.
If Augustine died.
Would he take her place downstairs in the bed next to Mathilde, would he sleep with her, is that the way it would be.
He hated himself.
The question remained, he didn't know how to get rid of it.

* * *

And so, in all likelihood it was superstition that made him do it. He was too afraid.
That the thought would kill Augustine.
That he'd be too forceful about it.
And so, he took Mathilde, before anything happened.
Not at night, because she was never alone.
During the day. In the woods.
She was picking up the logs he'd been cutting, piling them into the skeletal remains of a metal wheelbarrow. He stared at her for a long time.
Mathilde.
She looked up.
Mathilde.
And from the way she looked at him, from the pointless way she recoiled, he saw that she had understood.

* * *

Of course, it could have happened differently.
If only she had wanted it.
But, for months, Mathilde had never approached him.

Never made a gesture, a hint of tenderness. Had never given him any opening, and yet it was inevitable, he thought: there were only the two of them now. One time, Corentin had ventured to say something to this effect, but she pretended not to hear. She was still in mourning for her children, her life had stopped at that point; and clearly she too did not know why she had survived, why she happened to be in this place now, with this man she did not love and this old woman who was about to die. And that was the injustice: surviving.

But even with the desire not to see, not to hear, it was inextricable: in the Forests, they were all that was left, one woman and one man (Augustine did not count in this respect). It was blindingly obvious that something would happen. It was impossible to put a man and a woman on a desert island for months and for nothing to happen. It wasn't so much about desire, but instinct. It wasn't so much a human instinct, but an animal one, buried deep in the body and the mind; the void was unbearable, it must be filled.

But it was the way.

Corentin had fervently hoped that it would happen in another way. Had fervently hoped that Mathilde would be feeling the same reckless impulse.

He did it because the momentum in his guts was too strong.

He did it with tears in his eyes, because he knew it would be painful, to her for a start, and to him, for forcing her—this wasn't who he was, this animal putting his hand on her and not letting go, it was the world that left him no choice.

* * *

And Mathilde, yes, on that day she had seen in Corentin's eyes what was coming, and she was frightened.

She cried out but why, to whom—no one could hear.

She struggled.

Don't do this, please.

She heard her name on his lips, making up excuses, she felt the hard, knotty arms establishing their grip, and the voice breathing, be quiet, be quiet, please. Mathilde this isn't me. Mathilde we're going to die if we go on like this.

She began weeping. She had the big wide-open eyes of a mouse in a cat's paws, trying to escape and knowing it's already futile, she had the same terror of something ending, and she knew that Corentin would not kill her, but it was an identical sensation, an infinitesimal disappearance that no one would notice, a stifling, a fading.

And it was futile to weep, to beg, it had already been set in motion.

And so she stopped.

The world must be remade. Life must begin again.

She tried to think about something else.

Afterwards, never mind that she stopped going to help him.

Never mind that she stuck right by Augustine.

Never mind that she tried to keep away from him as much as she could—a time always came when she was alone, and he was always there.

She would see him coming and look at him with the gaze of a frightened little animal. He erased her gaze with a gesture.

She didn't try to flee, she no longer tried to push him away. All of that was useless.

She didn't say anything.

She waited.

Let him get it over with, remaking the world.

* * *

He tried to love her. And surely he did love her, in his way, the one required by exceptional circumstances, and surely the wound of childhood had come between them again, too. Do you remember when we wanted to get married, he murmured in her ear as he lay on top of her, she didn't reply that she had never wanted him, and yet he was handsome, Corentin, it was like a misunderstanding, a sad mistake, all of it, she didn't know what to say.

He wanted to cuddle her, he wanted to caress her body, that

softness the catastrophe had spared. He ran his hands over her, played with her skin. She grabbed his arm, angrily.

Do what you want. But do it quickly.

Then he knew she would hate him relentlessly.

He knew he would always be the very thing he had hoped not to be—a bastard and a rapist.

* * *

At night, wrapped in his blanket, he wept very quietly. At night, he was the one who prayed; he could see it wasn't working. Everything was slipping from him—Augustine's life, Mathilde's love. There were only three of them and they managed to hate one another, at best to ignore one another. What on earth was this human race, what did it carry within, basically, other than simply spite and nastiness, but he had his share, he even wondered if it was not worse in the Forests since he had come back.

That is why he worked like crazy, to convince himself that there was a reason and a usefulness to his presence; he worked or went into the Little Town, and, in the evening, he collapsed with no strength left to think, and it was better that way.

As the weeks passed, he realized that he no longer really saw the other two either. He feared Augustine's age and death, he feared Mathilde's scorn and hatred.

Why had he forced Mathilde—why did he go on doing it.

None of the explanations were satisfactory.

He wasn't a bastard. He suffered, he wanted her to love him, at least a little.

He suffered, but he lay in wait for her, took her by the arm. For all that she implored him—whatever she said, he led her into the woods.

Because he had to.

Not for him, not for her.

They needed children in the world.

Without children, it would all go dark.

* * *

After three months had gone by, Mathilde realized she was pregnant. And then Corentin no longer had access to her body—when he tried to touch her, she scratched her throat with her nails, let out such shrill screams that he was afraid even Augustine might hear.

Mathilde jabbed at her belly with her fingers to show him.

This is what you wanted. This is it. Now, go away. You'll come back when it's born. But until that day, don't you even try.

Mathilde.

You heard me.

Mathilde.

Die for all I care.

What in previous years had been winter was due to return. But was it so very different from that strange summer and strange autumn, when they were obliged to keep the embers going all day long in the wood stove or the fireplace to keep warm, when the sky was unremittingly gray and low, when the acid rain sometimes mixed with snowflakes that no one could find pleasure in—was it better or worse, having only one sea-son—uniform, drab, damp, a life sentence.

That's it, Corentin said to himself: in for life.

The sensation overwhelmed him when he awoke and every morning was so identical to the one before, and his eyes watered because there was so little light, and his heart closed because it was unthinkable that there might never again be any photosynthesis, or grass growing, or the river running clear, or Mathilde smiling at him.

But Augustine still loved him.

Augustine loved him, and Blind Boy did.

(But Blind Boy loved everyone—he loved Mathilde, too.)

He was almost fully grown now. Corentin had not got it wrong: the dog had become huge. He could have been harnessed to a cart if he'd been a bit less capricious, but for the time being, he was too dangerous. A puff of air, an illusion, and he was off like a lunatic. There were times when Corentin thought that something in his mind had been affected by the catastrophe. There was a sort of madness in his blank stare. A sort of uncontrollable joyousness, but who knew whether it could turn into full-scale insanity.

He disappeared. Sometimes for several days.

The first time he ran away—Corentin thought he'd died.

It was a real blow to the heart. He'd become attached to the dog.

* * *

He kept a close watch on the roundness of Mathilde's figure. She wore clothes that were too big, so they wouldn't be tight, or so that you couldn't see her shape, whatever—there it was, her clothes were loose, ample, huge. When the wind pressed her long sweaters against her skin, Corentin could make out her belly, starting to bulge.

He quivered with impatience. Nine months, it seemed forever. He wanted to see. He wanted it to become real, to mewl and cry.

But above all he was afraid.

That there would never be a birth, only the labor of blood and pain that terrified him in his dreams. He feared more than anything that the thing would go after the child as it had done that first time. He imagined it as a sort of monster endowed with consciousness, seeking humans out to devour them. A monster that went after and caught them. He knew he was wrong. The thing had gone through there and hadn't come back. But it had left enough poison in the air and on the earth to kill the last one alive.

What was there in Mathilde's belly now was, according to the thing, against nature. Mathilde was what the thing had methodically sought to destroy over these last months. She was the enemy. Corentin wished he could erase the Forests from the world and make them invisible, to protect them. He wished he could build insurmountable walls to keep them safe. And he would have, if he'd had the slightest grain of hope that it wouldn't be completely useless.

He was building their nest without realizing, the way an animal would. He spent more time draft-proofing the broken window panes, brought the reserves of firewood closer to the house, checked to make sure the temperature indoors stayed regular. He told Mathilde to help herself to cookies and choco-late, anything that made her happy. He built a new screen to give her more privacy from Augustine, he inventoried the household linens, asked what might be missing.

He was getting ready.

Unspeakably anxious, he awaited the arrival of a new human being.

* * *

On the far side of fear, Mathilde was alive. Deep inside her, snatches of happiness were working their way through, against her will. In the beginning she had fought, she was ashamed. So little time had gone by since the day everything had been swept away. There was still so much sorrow. Then she knew she had to build a future for the little creature sleeping in her belly. She forgot Corentin. She behaved as if the child were her hus-band's, and it was to him she dedicated the tiny moments of joy that sometimes went through her. She also offered them to her dead children—a little brother, a little sister is coming, she whispered to herself at night, and told them: what are we going to call it, how are we going to bring it up? Will it look like you?

Bit by bit, life resumed. Mathilde let the images of the past go blurry, mixed them with what was growing in her belly, pain gave way to the future. Sometimes it was difficult. Sometimes the joy of giving birth prevailed over everything. All that mattered was the child. It would be hers. It belonged to her.

Her little one.

She remembered the first time.

How she missed it now. There had been that urgency.

She didn't think about the thing. She didn't think about the fears that haunted Corentin—death, deformity, the birth of a monster.

All she knew was that they would have to be strong, both of them, mother and child. To give herself courage, she placed her hands on her belly and sang.

* * *

During the weeks of deep winter when they could not go out, during those terrible little months when at night the snow fell halfway up the windows and they had to fight to get the door open in the morning, Corentin sorted through their stocks of food. He wrote everything down. He put the supplies back according to date, trying to vary the terrible routine that lay ahead.

Cans. Jars. Starches.

Anything else, all gone.

He'd taken the overripe fruit from the shops and cooked them for half a day. Augustine made preserves that tasted of strained stewed fruit and old sugar. It was mediocre. Once they finished their cans of fruit in syrup, and their bellies rumbled with hunger, they'd be glad of the preserves.

Corentin went back to the town to take all the water and powdered milk he could find—in pharmacies, supermarkets, houses. For the unborn child, he had stepped over corpses in their houses, had searched through cupboards above burned gazes. He wasn't ashamed. He thanked them as he left. He always closed the door behind him, as if someone still lived there.

Augustine's expression had changed.

She, too, was waiting for the baby. She had noticed—Mathilde hadn't said anything.

When Corentin wasn't there, they talked about next summer and the birth, almost laughing. It was a little star coming back. They mustn't think about sadness. They mustn't look at the gray earth.

Augustine was jubilant.

At last, she knew why she was still here, alive.

She had the knowledge of children in her hands. In this country, now blackened and melancholy, she'd brought plenty of them into the world, before hospitals existed, before they got this far—more than a thousand.

Corentin had decided he would empty the little town of every last thing that could be of use to them. He went there once or twice a week. He obsessed about it. He made a sketch of the town, the streets, each block of houses. He explored them methodically, block by block, building by building, room by room. He circled the territory he'd already covered with a pencil, crossing it off in red. He would delineate other neighborhoods in blue, for next time.

He took everything. The thought of lacking anything terrified him.

It was old people who were afraid of lacking.

And him.

He'd become old.

In his filthy coat, and his filthy trousers, his shoes covered with mud or snow. His hair, too long—he looked like a tramp.

His cart and his dog.

A nutcase.

If he could have seen himself, that's what he would have said. Before.

Now, you couldn't say anything anymore. You just had to survive, and to survive in this world, you had to be completely crazy.

* * *

And so, he eventually worked it out. Two years, three months, and twenty-seven days.

If they were careful.

Two years, three months, and twenty-seven days' worth of food.

Always the same.

But they no longer ate for pleasure. They ate to endure.

With their fingers, because there wasn't enough water to wash cutlery. They stopped using it. They each had their own plate, which they used over and over, every day. And their own napkin to wipe it clean. Augustine had made a knot in hers to know which one, because they were all the same, red and white checks. Mathilde folded hers into a triangle. Corentin rolled his up in a ball.

Once a week, he went to the stream and brought back two big buckets of water. The stream was far below. Coming back up was hell on his lungs. He put the water on to boil in a pot, on the wood-burning stove they also used for heat—they didn't light a fire in the fireplace until the end of the day, and then only on very cold days, to save on logs.

With this boiling water, which they saw as a treasure, they rinsed the plates and napkins, and a few items of clothing, all in the same basin. Corentin made a first attempt at having a wash and it didn't burn. So now they took three bottles each, old Pommard bottles with faded labels, and filled them with hot water. They took their turns in the shower. It gave them an unreal sensation of cleanliness.

They didn't drink the water. Corentin didn't want to, he couldn't be sure. Nothing had come back to the stream. Even though they boiled it, he was afraid.

Two years, three months, and twenty-seven days—and then what.

Were there still any edible roots underground.

Would the seeds in packets that had overheated in the stores sprout all the same.

Corentin didn't want to think about it. He only saw the respite.

He knew he hadn't explored everything in the little town. There were some things left.

Mathilde's belly looked like a sun.

* * *

At the end of winter, on the road that led to the Little Town, the one he always took, he encountered some survivors. When he saw them a few hundred yards ahead of him, he was frightened. Blind Boy growled and Corentin caught him by the scruff of his neck—he must remember to make a collar for him, in case he tried to get away and run after something, Corentin couldn't hold him back, he felt his fingers slipping over his smooth fur, his thick muscles.

There were seven of them. Adults.

All the children are dead, thought Corentin. Children were too fragile. There are none left anywhere—except in Mathilde's belly.

The survivors had stopped by the side of the road. They were frightened of the dog.

Corentin quickly looped a rope around Blind Boy's neck and yanked.

Easy!

The hoarse growl that came from Blind Boy's throat was terrifying. Even though he knew his dog inside out, Corentin was anxious. He made a gesture with his hand, but Blind Boy's forward tugging nearly knocked him over. He caught himself just in time. They would soon weigh the same thing, dog and master. He shouted again.

Easy!

Corentin was the one who went up to them. When he was a few feet away, they recoiled.

The dog, they said.

I've got him.

They looked at each other with genuine fascination. They had all survived—the seven of them, and Corentin, and Blind Boy. They studied every face, every body, for an explanation. Who were they to still be alive, where had they been at the instant of the catastrophe—in hiding places, niches, microsystems that had protected them. Gradually, fear gave way to incredulous joy.

We are not alone.

But they didn't know what to say. They didn't know how to talk to each other, what questions to ask. Before, they would have asked about professions, described their homes, their passions, their children. All of that had vanished.

Five men and two women, and then nothing.

They might have been able to qualify the thing, hope that one of them knew, and would explain, that at last they would understand what had happened.

But what good would it do, going back over it.

All that existed was a very fragile future.

So Corentin simply asked which way they were headed.

West.

Apparently in the west it's not as cold.

Apparently in the west there are survivors gathering all along the sea, that there are still things to be done there. But it's a long way. And you?

Corentin shook his head. I'm staying here.

Don't you want to come with us, with your dog and your rifle.

I have a woman. She's expecting a baby, soon. She can't start on a long trip now.

We plan to have children, too. But we want to get to the west first.

I see. Maybe we'll go, later.

You'd be welcome, with your child, and the dog, and the rifle.

They didn't say how they would get to the west. Corentin

didn't ask. The west was a hope. They would find it if they were destined to. Otherwise, they would keep walking indefinitely.

Do you have anything to eat?

The request caught Corentin unawares and he stiffened.

He had a full cart behind him. He'd covered it with a tarp because of the drizzle. He alone knew what was underneath—blankets, more clothes, empty jerrycans, a few gardening tools. And then there were cans of food, packets of flour, sugar, and pasta. Melba toasts. Jam. He alone knew, but they could see the cart was filled to overflowing.

He kept silent, thinking about all that.

The others understood. They didn't say anything.

You must have gone through towns, Corentin remarked, after a long moment.

It was all empty. Maybe people who'd been through there took everything. We don't have much to eat.

Not to make it all the way to the west.

No. Not to make it to the west.

The figure was dancing in Corentin's head. Two years, five months, and three days' worth of supplies—since he wouldn't rest until he'd found all the supplies in every nook and cranny of the town and since, day after day, he'd brought back more than what they were eating.

But it wouldn't last. He'd reached the last neighborhoods in the town. Before long, they would have to start on their reserves and everything would begin to go down.

The food in the cart, however, hadn't been counted. It wouldn't mean less for them. There would still be two years, five months, and three days.

And besides, he didn't have to give them everything.

He could also let Blind Boy off the leash; he was quiet, but he could feel him pulling against the rope.

He looked at them.

They weren't threatening him.

It doesn't matter, said one of the men.

Wait.

Corentin pulled back the tarp and shared what he had piled in the cart. As he was apportioning the food, he could sense the emotion on their faces, and he felt happy. He made two equal piles, one which he put back in the cart, and one which he left by the side of the road for them.

There you go.

They practically ran to get it.

They shared out several packets, devouring everything while urging one another to keep some for later. One of the women was crying.

Corentin went around them to continue on his way.

They thanked him and he gave a wave of his hand.

A wave goodbye, a wave that meant, It's nothing, but that wasn't true—it wasn't nothing.

Thanks, they said again.

A bit further along, he paused. He was worried they might be watching what direction he was headed in.

What if they followed him. What if they decided to steal everything from him after all.

But they picked up all the food he'd given them and headed west.

Corentin still waited, for a long while. Until they had vanished beyond the last bend, the last burned valley; he waited patiently.

Only then did he let Blind Boy go, and he went back up to the Forests.

The date in his notebook said March 17.

Corentin thought of crocuses and snowdrops. He thought of the places where they grew—every year when winter was over, ever since his mother had left him in the Forests like a burdensome package.

He hadn't even gone to look.

He hadn't even wondered whether Marie had survived the thing. He thought about it one day, more or less by chance. The question occurred to him, entered his mind, then went out again. It wasn't that important. Marie wasn't part of his life.

But the catastrophe that had devoured the crocuses and snowdrops—that catastrophe was really there, and he really hated it.

Eight months now.

A billion years.

All three of them—Augustine, Mathilde, and Corentin— had forgotten that the landscape could be anything other than gray and brown and barren. They'd forgotten colors. They'd forgotten the sun.

It's normal, thought Corentin. March is too soon. It was the same, before.

That's why he hadn't gone to look: not to succumb to despair yet again. Not to stifle the quiver he felt inside, and which he didn't dare question, for fear of spooking it.

Because there was a strange effervescence among them, not unlike the impatience of springtime, when something from the earth began to rise in the trees and in animals and in people. Something that gave a rush of blood and vigor, that readied the seasons, the sowing and harvesting, of fields of wheat and apple trees, and yes it was a long way off, but it was slowly coming and everybody, all three of them, could feel it.

Suddenly, in this broken place, it was beginning again.

It was starting up.

Not one of them said as much—out of superstition, not to jinx it. But the way they looked outside, the way they studied the view out the window every morning, and checked the sky: the same thing was piercing their guts.

That spring would be here.

There were no actual signs. They were still gripped by cold at dawn, the rain soaked the paths and eventually caused the walls inside the house to seep, despite the fire and the warmth. The sky was overcast. If any birds did fly over, they wouldn't see them. Corentin thought he could hear them and opened his eyes wide, in vain. Gray monotony had been steadily crushing them, these eight months. That hadn't changed, either.

It was inside them.

An instinct.

And they were animals, too, there was this momentum that wasn't usual for them, it was something animal, visceral, murmuring that everything would start up again.

They couldn't be wrong.

It would explode all of a sudden, they were sure of it.

They waited.

They checked for clues—a cuckoo calling, buds appearing on a branch, something soft in the air. They thought the meadows might be covered with a fine green cloak.

But it was just from so much looking and listening. They thought they could see and they thought they could hear.

They went down to the stream. It was too cold to put their feet in—and would they have dared, anyway, because they still couldn't see any living creatures, it was only the water itself that caused the stream to stir, and the banks were black.

They had to wait some more.

But it was April, and everything was the same.

It was May, and nothing appeared.

There was no spring.

* * *

When he wrote the date June 1 in his notebook, Corentin held his face in his hands. It was hard. It was painful. His body was suffering from the lack of sunlight and warmth; his mind was failing him. It was as if it were raining inside his very eyes, as if the torrents that had fallen for months were flowing through his eyelids.

He looked at Augustine and he looked at Mathilde.

Their white skin, like ghosts.

The only color: Mathilde's blue eyes; the purple shadows they all wore under their eyes.

Augustine, as if completely transparent. Already evaporated. She had stopped mending her dishrag, her fingers had worn through it from holding it so much.

Mathilde's round belly.

And the days, all the same.

The world had stopped moving forward.

Only they themselves changed. Week after week, more pale and fragile and sad. Nauseated by the same cans of food, the same smells, the same gestures to light the stove and shovel to clear the blocked drain when the rainwater came up to the door of the house; they went around in circles, they waited.

They each had their own spot in the house, it had simply worked out that way. Mathilde and Augustine sat in the kitchen where it was warm—sometimes on the sofa, when they felt too stiff. Corentin sat with his back to the fire, curled up in an armchair.

Blind Boy didn't come inside. He couldn't stand being shut indoors.

Corentin took him to the woods. He went on hoping. He would think about this hope before he went out, to give it some strength.

Find a blade of grass, a leaf, a stem. A trace of rebirth.

Coming home disappointed, every time. He tried to reason with himself, found convincing arguments: it was just a question of time. It was too cold, it was too damp. Too windy. He wanted to help nature, and he would scratch the ground looking for a chestnut, an acorn, a hazelnut. The husks he found were soft and empty. There was nothing he could replant, nothing that might sprout.

Sometimes he could feel a sticky lump of dejection in his chest. What if there was nothing left, to get the world going again.

But the world had always kept going, extinctions were never total.

It had always taken time, that was all.

It had taken one or two or ten million years.

A little hope, a tiny little hope.

On June 14, toward the end of the morning, Mathilde's waters broke.

S he knew it would be hard. She'd prepared herself for it. Augustine had prepared her. Nevertheless, she was afraid and her gaze was unsteady as she looked around her for the old woman. Her only lifeline.

It will be all right.

She nodded her head, not really believing it. It was very different now that it was happening. She knew about labor. But she also knew nothing about it, because this time it would be so different. Like for animals. As if she were in the wild. That was what she had become, she thought: feral.

The first time it had been very painful.

And this morning, when there'd be nothing to help her, she hardly dared imagine.

Like before, Augustine had said.

But before, there were shots.

Before that before.

It will be all right, Augustine said again, bringing hot water and towels, her eyes shining, a vitality restored to her from God knows where.

Mathilde gave her a wan smile.

In actual fact, she was convulsed with apprehension. She felt something enormous inside her. She tried to tell herself that this was normal: there really was something in her belly, it was alive, and stirring, it found the space too small now and was demanding to be let out. But there was also foreboding.

It's going to be hard.

The feeling wouldn't leave her. She could take it, she wasn't the fearful type.

She'd never had any foreboding before.

So, naturally.

* * *

Stay here, Augustine ordered Corentin.

He was getting ready to go out, to leave the house to the women. Blind Boy was waiting, silently begging for an extra walk. Corentin hesitated.

I don't think so . . .

Come here. You have to stay here. For the next time.

And he also felt that anxiety that was gluing him to the spot, he couldn't think, he couldn't answer back, tell Augustine that she would be there for the next time, or that he was afraid of blood. He didn't dare say it.

He stayed.

Oh, the ordeal.

For Mathilde. For him.

He was useless. Probably Augustine had thought he'd watch so that he'd learn, but he just couldn't.

There was too much screaming. The screams made him weep and wring his hands.

He hung his head, he stared at the floor.

Through the French door, he could see the dog, attentive, he wished he could grab his fur with both hands to keep himself from trembling.

Yes, the screaming was enough.

He knew it was normal, in the beginning.

But this wasn't the beginning anymore and it wasn't normal anymore.

Hours had gone by. There was something wrong.

Sometimes he would look up at the sky, in a mixture of rage

and fear, and he would pray. He'd thought he would never do it again. But prayer was all that was left. Every other solution had vanished.

Mathilde was going to die, was what he suddenly feared, and he was praying, off in a corner of the room to keep out of Augustine's way as she came and went, his arms wrapped around himself.

Not to see.

You're a coward, he thought.

But he couldn't. He concentrated on staring at the wall across from him, or at the floor, or at Blind Boy on the other side of the door. At Augustine, who'd been bustling about for far too long.

Augustine, with her troubled face. Her troubled gaze when she trained it on him.

This time, you have to help me.

At first, he didn't understand. The words didn't reach him. He said, Yes.

Augustine dragged him by the arm, forcefully leading him to the bed.

She said it again: And now you have to help me.

And he saw.

* * *

Mathilde's eyes were half open, but she didn't recognize him. She was elsewhere. Too tired, too much pain. No one could imagine, no one could put themselves in her position. The pain obliterated every thought, filled her entire brain. There was nothing else. Mathilde would have done anything to be rid of it, including piercing her heart with a knife. Augustine didn't have the strength to stop her.

When he saw her bloodless face and the sheets stained with blood and sweat, Corentin recoiled. He had to close his eyes to steady himself—to stop the dizziness and not throw up.

Corentin.

Augustine, I can't.

It is not looking good and I need you. So you have to open your eyes, and you have to do as I tell you.

I can't . . .

You are going to obey me. That's it. Just do what I tell you.

He glanced up at Mathilde. She looked like a dead woman—but one who is suffering terribly. Augustine was just as pale.

* * *

So this is what it meant, giving birth.

This horrible experience.

Augustine was pressing Mathilde's belly, kneading her flesh, encouraging her in a soft voice. And she, the mother-to-be, her hands clutching the sheets as if she wanted to tear them, screaming that it had to stop, that it hurt, it hurt, it hurt. Augustine stroked her brow. Then went back to the huge, bluish belly.

That's good, my girl. Go on. It's turning around in the right direction.

But it wasn't good, thought Corentin next to her, on the verge of passing out, his hands, too, sticky with blood and some strange liquid, mechanically carrying out Augustine's orders. There was nothing good about this pain that wouldn't end, and this baby that wouldn't come. And who could blame it, really, for not leaving the womb, what was there to see in this world—why had he, Corentin, done this, why had he engendered so much suffering, so many screams, for the sake of what illusion, what lie?

He caught his breath whenever Mathilde did. Her breathing set the pace for his own. When she stopped breathing, he felt stifled. Her legs convulsed—Corentin trembled, staggered, caught himself on the bed. He didn't look at her. It was too much for him. This wasn't Mathilde. This wasn't the woman he loved in silence and in vain. He refused to see her in this twisted, wounded thing.

Time passed in a sort of dazed trance, everything buzzing around them. A veil seemed to have bound Corentin's ears. Sounds were muted; he felt dizzy. Through the door, he could see that Blind Boy had not left his post. Night was falling. Mathilde's cries were not as loud.

At first, he thought she was in less pain but—he felt her freeing herself. She was leaving. Corentin's hands slid over her skin, she was fleeing.

He didn't know how to hold her back.

Mathilde, Mathilde.

Bit by bit she had stopped struggling against the little creature that was ravaging her body. In the end, she had found only one way to get rid of the pain: to die with it.

Augustine slapped her and Corentin gave a start.

Speak to her. We're nearly there.

And he hunted for the right words to say to this shape— hardly a woman anymore, this pile of terrified flesh begging to be left alone, and as he went even closer, leaning over her, suddenly her eyes met his.

Please.

There was no more noise, no more screaming.

No more movement.

As if the house were dead. On the other side of the door, Blind Boy was listening and couldn't hear anything. Beyond the walls it was like a tomb.

There were smells. Too strong to be pleasant.

The dog pressed his nose up against a patch of window, making a circle with his breath. His ears were pricked forward. He hesitated to push against the door. He hesitated to bark. The silence, the immobility were unsettling. From where he was, he could just make out Augustine's shape, collapsed in an armchair. She wasn't moving.

Is that how humans sleep.

He waited some more.

Night had fallen, it was cold. It didn't bother him. He was a little hungry, but he didn't protest. He sighed a few times—a way of signaling his bewilderment.

The sky was black, like every night. No stars, no moon lighting up the countryside. Blind Boy didn't mind; he could see as if it were day. He saw the way he always did, gray and white, a long veil covering his retina. His eyes were his ears and nose. He'd grown used to it.

But not to this silence.

He turned his head, thought he heard something. He sniffed. Breathed out.

Well.

He eventually went a little farther away. An old instinct: to go hunting. But there wasn't even the meanest shrew to catch. And even if there were. He put his nose to the ground and prowled for a moment. Circles. Ovals. A meandering that constantly led him back to the house, not to miss anything, should something happen.

And there was something.

Like a whimper.

For a fraction of a second Blind Boy thought it was coming from outside, a creature nearby, and he froze, his ears moving in every direction.

But it wasn't.

It was in the house.

With a vigor that stirred up the black leaves around him, he ran back.

* * *

Corentin got up, in spite of his headache and nausea. For him too, it was because of the noise.

But it wasn't a whimper.

It was a cry. A wail. The sound of a newborn baby.

He leaned over to lift it up from the bed, by Mathilde. A murmur.

Hey.

The child was silent.

Corentin took a few steps, soothing it, leaving Mathilde motionless, walking past Augustine who was gently snoring, exhausted. He saw the dog at the door. And, of course, it was silly, but Blind Boy was the only one who didn't know, the only one he could tell. So he smiled, and through the glass he showed him the baby, which had nodded off again.

* * *

And they had come that close.

They'd very nearly.

Failed, given up—died. All of them.

It was only a matter of what: a few minutes, a few seconds. Before exhaustion and helplessness would have gotten the better of them.

At last, the child was born.

Mathilde's suffering did not stop, however, even then.

Augustine had washed and dressed the little boy; it wasn't crying. Corentin held Mathilde's hand—for the first time, she didn't pull it away.

She wasn't smiling. She wasn't feeling better.

She just said, It still hurts.

That's normal, whispered Augustine.

It hurts as much as before.

Corentin placed a hot towel over her belly, to ease the spasms. In vain. She wanted to take the baby, and couldn't. Even the blanket was too heavy on her body. Augustine made her swallow a sip of rum, she had to get warm now, she had to relax. Mathilde threw up.

And then suddenly she cried out. This terrifying thing, which none of them had been prepared to hear.

It's starting again.

* * *

Corentin carefully set the baby down next to Mathilde, whose eyes were slightly open. She murmured, almost inaudibly.

Tired.

Everything is all right, said Corentin, quietly.

Are they here?

Both of them. They're sleeping. You get some sleep now, too.

She ran her hand over the sheet until she could feel them near her. The little boy on her left, the little girl on her right. Herself in the middle. An exhausted but vigilant sentry—she smiled, and fell into a deep sleep.

Corentin looked at the twins.

They weren't nice to look at. They were wrinkled, scowling, ugly. But so endearing. The flesh of his flesh. It had a strange effect on him, made his eyes shine.

Papa, he said. I'm your papa.

When he went out, Blind Boy licked his hand and gave him a strange look.

Looked at him a bit to one side—so then Corentin murmured a few words and the dog raised his head toward his voice, and Corentin got the feeling he could actually see him.

It was a strange day.

He looked at the sky. Total darkness. Still no stars, and he was sorry: it would have been the right evening for stars. It would have been a fine gift.

He pulled his jacket tighter around him and fed Blind Boy.

He said, There you go.

He thought of the babies sleeping in the bed with Mathilde. The world was slowly starting up again. The world had a future. And Corentin had a great fear. It was too late to wonder about it, of course, but he knew that good and evil always go hand in hand. Positive and negative. Joy and distress.

He had two children now.

And that was joy.

He listened to the silence of the night. Remembering the night calls of owls, nightingales, crickets; it was too deeply rooted in his memory to have vanished already, he thought he could hear them, was briefly lulled.

And then there was distress.

A world where his children would never know the call of owls, nightingales, or crickets.

Or the color of flowers, or the hot breath of the sun. Or the silvery glinting of fish in a river, or the pale, wind-tossed specks of pollen in a summer's late-afternoon light; or the taste of raspberries crushed in your hand, or of the cherry plums and greengages you've fought the wasps over.

No doubt they would never see a car or a television working. They'd look at their parents with surprise when they talked about electricity and running water, they wouldn't understand how people made use of them, before. They wouldn't understand, either, what an airplane was, or a sheep, or the sea, or music.

It would all be difficult. It would all take a long time. Everything would seem impossible.

They'd grow up with no other living people around them. They wouldn't know that, before, there used to be billions of them on the planet.

Too many, wanting too much.

And now—a few scattered survivors.

Suddenly, it was unthinkable, to bring a child into the world.

Two children.

Why, why?

So that two years and five months from now they wouldn't be able to feed them anymore?

Corentin took his head in his hands: this wasn't the time to be wondering about things like this, he was exhausted, stunned, still trembling.

He had to see the joy of it.

The joy was that something living had come. He had enough to feed them for two years.

After that, they'd see.

After that, maybe the world would have done the same as

Mathilde's belly: it would have recovered. It would have started growing again. It had to.

But deep down, Corentin didn't know.

He didn't know a thing.

He could only come up with idle theories, and were his choices anything different—subjective, chance reasoning—wagers, that's what they were, their existence was founded on wagers and on luck.

To believe in luck after what had happened was just so absurd.

To force the hand of destiny when there was no more destiny.

But Corentin made himself.

He had to do things one after the other.

For the time being, he had enough to feed them all, to heat the house. They were in a safe place. He worried more about the water.

So, he'd see to the water.

Tomorrow.

But tomorrow wouldn't be the way he imagined.

Tomorrow would bring him up short.

It would be a day of real, of great sorrow.

It would leave him with a bitter taste in his mouth, and the certainty that what would save them, in this new world that had nothing to offer, would be their ability to curve their spines, to weather the blows, and like old people—to fall to the ground, be trampled on, and get up again in spite of everything, not too quickly, not to ruffle fate, not too loudly, so as not to attract attention, but get up again all the same, always.

But in the meantime, God it hurt.

When Corentin woke up, when he saw Augustine, who hadn't moved from her armchair, he knew straightaway, some sort of irrepressible instinct informing him, that she was dead.

For a few hours, there had been five of them in the world. Then there were only four.

Augustine left a huge gap.

The irreparable sin: they were the ones who had killed her—with their inability to bring into the world children unwilling to come, with their recklessness, their blindness. They had thought only of themselves. Augustine didn't mind, of course. And yet no doubt she knew what would happen. She had surely assessed the strength of her skeletal arms, her exhausted heart, her slowing pulse. Did she ignore the fact that the two little births would be too much for her—no, a dozen times no, she must have seen it coming. And, as always, she kept silent.

* * *

Mathilde came with the babies in her arms to the edge of the pit Corentin had dug at the end of the garden. He had lowered his great-grandmother's body, wrapped in a sheet, and covered the shroud with earth. After the last shovelful, he burst into tears.

Mathilde came, her eyes were red.

Corentin leaned on the shovel. The words were in his chest, too heavy. He stayed silent. Mathilde murmured a prayer, then said how cold it was. She wanted them all to go back. Corentin shook his head.

A little longer.

It was the last time.

Next, he would finish leveling the ground, and where a moment before there had been Augustine, now all that remained was a mound of earth. He didn't even know whether the grass would grow again someday, whether he'd be able to plant some violets, because Augustine had once said that she would like violets on her grave.

Violets, and to see the sea.

And she'd had neither.

And it was pointless to shed tears over it, it was too late, it was pointless to feel sorry: Augustine would never see the sea.

I should have done something about it before, thought Corentin, filled with remorse. He could have taken her a hundred times when he was at the university. He didn't have time. Didn't take her. That would teach him a lesson. What had he thought—that Augustine would live forever?

You had to live every day as if it were your last—not to scare yourself, but to have as few regrets as possible. And no matter what, you'd always have some. And no matter what, there was no such thing as a perfect death.

Corentin went on kneeling on the damp earth, lost in thought.

Now he was responsible for the others, all of them. There was no one else to share it with, no one to bear part of the burden. No more advice. No more old hand on his shoulder to tell him he had to keep going, had to stop thinking. Just tiny, awkward little hands, that he would have to hold until they could make it on their own, until they would wave to say goodbye, since children always leave—but Augustine had said as much. For the time being, he had to stop going around in circles, stop thinking, it was like having regrets: it was pointless. But it was so hard not to.

* * *

They called them Altair and Electra.

Since they couldn't see the stars in the sky, they re-created them on earth.

The twins had clear blue eyes, diaphanous skin. The disappearance of the sun meant they were pale children, down to their faintly drawn fingernails, their near-white hair.

For a long time, Corentin was afraid they wouldn't survive. They didn't cry, didn't beg. They didn't eat much. As soon as they could, they spent their time staring out at the garden, looking for stones and naked trees, nodding their heads like old tortoises. They looked somehow unfinished—it wasn't true, but Corentin couldn't help thinking it, he kept looking for what might be wrong, observed them closely.

It was the slowness in the way they moved, or blinked, the effort they made to open their mouths only to have no sound come out. Their fixed gazes, their empty pupils. To Corentin, it was as if something had been overlooked—or was it their stupor upon discovering this near-dead universe, when they had expected a noisy, joyful planet, or anything but this, and he didn't dare mention it to Mathilde, didn't dare say that he thought they were abnormal, that the world was only good for engendering monsters.

So he kept his eye on them. But there was so little progress at the dawn of lives like theirs. Everything was in slow motion.

Their elongated eyes, their too-small lips. Their fingers, which couldn't catch or hold, their bodies that weren't getting longer or thicker, and yet Mathilde did have enough milk, hidden away in her breasts that had become enormous, he had touched them one night, and it took both his hands to circle each one of them, the skin was taut and swollen, distressingly soft. He went back to his bed and lay down, full of emotion.

He slept downstairs now on Mathilde's old mattress at the

other end of the room, while she shared Augustine's big bed with the infants.

The first time he approached her again and ran his hesitant fingers over her skin, she was silent, not to wake them. She put a finger to her lips. Don't make any noise.

So they did not make any noise.

Then she got into the habit of putting the twins in the little bed, and Corentin, suddenly finding himself in the double bed, with her disturbing nearness, had access to her more often. But did it mean she was giving her willing consent—he knew very well that it didn't. It was just easier. She didn't want the babies to wake up, that was all. She didn't want them to hear.

As for Corentin, she never looked at him. Conveyed nothing. She didn't try to elude him, either. At first, he'd thought that being together with her again would bring them closer, if for no other reason than need, loneliness. But nothing had changed: Mathilde waited—like nearly all females in nature. Sometimes, afterwards, she would get up and work on some sewing, or add a log to the stove, or move something that didn't need moving. It was her way of forgetting. Corentin tucked his head between his elbows and pretended to sleep. Pretended not to see her indifference. Mathilde's smiles were for Altair and Electra.

Corentin wasn't jealous.

Just sad—because he was always alone.

Sadness came, encircling his heart.

* * *

There were two rituals now. In the morning—walk through the garden to murmur a few words at Augustine's tomb. In the afternoon, take Blind Boy for a walk.

Blind Boy wasn't always there.

He would disappear. He'd come back in the evening, or the next day, or three days later.

Shit! Corentin exclaimed when he saw him, torn between relief and anger.

The dog didn't give a damn.

You know I don't like it when you disappear.

And off he'd go again.

Four days—and this time, when he came back, there was nothing but fury in Corentin's heart. Four days was too much. Four days meant four nights that fell on his absence, four empty dawns, and between them, endless questions. Was Blind Boy dead, or hurt, should he look everywhere for him, was it already too late? No way of being sure. No way not to think about it. And then there was this other fear: Blind Boy wasn't protecting them anymore. He had deserted. Just when they might need him the most, with two newborn babies, and the fatigue and dizziness of something huge and unknown—where was Blind Boy just then, what was he thinking, had he forgotten his role as a guard dog, a wild animal, a giant?

So Corentin shouted, and shouted loud. The dog turned his head the other way. And maybe under normal circumstances— maybe before, when the world was as it should be, it would have made Corentin laugh to see the animal sulking, dodging his reprimands, sighing because the man went on and on scolding him. But it wasn't like before, and Mathilde was like the dog, she turned her head and waited, and he couldn't take it anymore, he didn't want them to ignore him anymore, neither Mathilde nor the dog, and it filled him with anger and rage, he let it all come. He grabbed Blind Boy by the scruff to shake him, to clutch at his thick, strong hide, without warning, because he really couldn't stand it anymore, and everything, for a split second, had all melted together—the aloofness, the indifference, enough, and that was what he shouted, then, too—Enough!

But he couldn't tighten his grip. Couldn't move the dog. In

a flash, Blind Boy's teeth were on his arm. Corentin had no time to do anything. Couldn't move, or get away. He didn't even see it coming. It happened too quickly.

He felt the pain, he felt the fangs in his flesh. With one tug of his jaw Blind Boy would have the strength to tear his muscles and bones and tendons.

But that's not what happened.

Instead, Corentin's eyes saw the dog's blank gaze.

Blind Boy could see him—there was such intensity in the opaque veil covering his eyes, such a threat. For a moment, Corentin was convinced he'd been mistaken all this time, that Blind Boy wasn't blind. And yet, he'd seen him stumble so often, bump into things.

No, the dog didn't see him.

But there could be no mistake: he knew what he held in his shining teeth. He knew what he was doing—or not doing.

Just keep holding tight.

Then slowly he relaxed his grip, and Corentin pressed his hands on the spots that were bleeding. He sat down next to the dog, trembling.

He murmured. I'm tired.

A sort of excuse, a helplessness.

They were silent for a long time.

Corentin would have liked to say more. He would have liked to get it out, for words to attach to this life that just kept on getting more and more lonely, with Blind Boy leaving, too, and Mathilde silently rejecting him, and the babies clinging to her breasts, there was no room for him, no room at all, he was just there to keep them warm and fed and to stay out of it, as if he were on the doorstep, as if he were behind an unbreakable pane of glass.

Corentin took Blind Boy to the stream. The water washed the tree roots, gleaming black in the eddies. Corentin tossed a stone, and it made a joyful sound; the currents flowed around it, the stream was eight inches deep, he could see the bed of brown and gray and yellow pebbles.

Before, moss and algae used to cling there.

The water was transparent. Corentin crouched down and scooped some up with his hand.

The water was dead.

He let it flow through his fingers.

The dog ran through the splashes he made.

Corentin eventually tossed pieces of wood into the stream, and he watched the dog playing. Blind Boy jumped, turned, rushed away, came back. It should have been amusing, but it was merely sad.

Joy, like Corentin in the house: it no longer had a place here.

He was tossing bits of wood, nothing more. Blind Boy fetched them.

He was there—he wasn't really there. His heart, his soul in a tomb. It weighed too heavily, midway between his gut and his chest, where everything was tight and trembling. So heavy he should have sat down, but if he sat down, he wouldn't get up, and if he didn't sit down, he would fall, because he was too weighty, too low, leaden and faltering. Too short of breath. There was sweat on his brow, yet it was still cold.

He said, Time to go back.

Just a murmur.

The dog went on playing.

Come on—the words tore at his lungs.

He turned his back to the stream, made it as if to start back up. Stopped to check whether Blind Boy was coming.

Then he saw him and cried out.

No!

The dog raised his head.

Don't do that, stop!

Corentin ran toward him.

Blind Boy was wagging his tail, indifferent to Corentin's concern, and started lapping the stream water again with great scoops of his tongue.

* * *

The dog didn't die.

How long he'd been drinking from the stream, Corentin would never know. But the main thing was that the water was no longer toxic.

He went and gazed at it for long stretches of time. Maybe he was waiting for something living to emerge, and it didn't, because everything had been killed. It doesn't matter, he thought. It's no longer poisonous. It's empty, and nothing else.

He gazed at it, and let some time go by. He listened to the burbling and eddying and gurgling, the currents that rushed against the banks then continued on their way in curls of foam; he put his hand in the water until the cold of it burned. In the end, he decided to fill a bucket.

He boiled the water and drank some, too. Not much: one swallow. That evening, half a glass.

He slept badly, watching out for signs of burning, discomfort, asphyxiation.

He didn't die, either.

* * *

Altair and Electra were playing in the garden.

They couldn't walk yet, they were crawling. Blind Boy didn't leave their side, and whenever they went beyond the limits of the former vegetable garden, he coaxed them back with his muzzle.

The signs that had worried Corentin had gradually vanished. There was nothing left of the twins' slowness from those first months. It had taken time, that was all.

Time to unfold, like wrinkled clothing eventually taken from the drawer, with the traces of its long rest.

Time to tame a new world, to define its contours and characteristics, to learn about it, and agree to settle there.

Maybe they still lacked strength. Maybe they lacked sunshine and a varied diet. They still had very pale skin and slender bodies, unusual in small infants. But they had become what Corentin had dreamt of: vibrant, joyful creatures, and this astonished him. There were times he couldn't understand why they were laughing, or babbling and waving their hands, he wondered what could be making the pair of them so happy, he wished he could be in their minds, in their language.

He had given up, but to see them and hear them—this, he often reminded himself, this was joy.

They played without toys, they played with what the world had left behind. They would toss handfuls of earth around them. When it landed on their heads, Corentin could hear their giggling all the way from the woods where he was stripping the bark from branches of chestnut. Their laughter, the first time, had seized him. He just listened, to be sure. Transfixed. Children laughing.

His children.

It was such a huge thing and so strange. Corentin had not heard laughter since the catastrophe. He had forgotten what it was like. A crystalline sound, very gentle and very clear, a trill like that of a bird, piercing the air, and finally: something infinitely cheerful.

After that, whenever the twins burst out laughing, no matter where he was, Corentin would stop to take his fill. He made it into a ritual, where time was suspended—the same sort of ritual as when he used to thrill to the sound of bells, before, when the angelus would ring seven o'clock, and he would look up for a few seconds from his work in the vegetable garden, or his homework, or his firewood chores.

Now he closed his eyes, and he listened.

And so, he thought that not everything was in vain, not everything was ugly. Sometimes it was very brief, sometimes the twins had fits of laughter that lasted several minutes, and Corentin was surprised to find himself laughing too, even though he couldn't see them, or know why, just from the sound of them, because it was contagious and the catastrophe hadn't changed anything in this regard, laughter restored life to them, he wiped his eyes, it was too much emotion. He caught his breath, reached for the ax. The babies' laughter stayed in his memory like a locket on a chain where you place the tiniest, most precious thing you own—a photograph, a lock of hair, a baby tooth. On sad days, Corentin opened his memory and listened to Altair and Electra's laughter.

* * *

The children had churned up the garden with their games, with their chubby little hands tossing dirt the way you toss confetti or stars. When he got home in the evening, Corentin looked at the black, turned soil: it was like some vacant lot, a field full of molehills, and it seemed alive. He didn't do anything with it, didn't hoe or rake. He stared at the minuscule craters and bumps, he stroked the ground with his fingertips. The seeds he'd found in nurseries after the catastrophe had not amounted to anything, just moldy little brown and white clumps. Let the children turn over the soil as much as they pleased.

Corentin leafed through the pages in his notebook and counted the days.

The days went by too quickly, whereas the hours seem endless.

The days were devouring their supplies of food, without adding anything new. He thought about it every night, it had become an obsession, how could it not. To eat was to live.

At that moment, they had one year and eight months left.

Before famine, when everything would end. And Corentin trembled even more at the time of day when darkness exacerbated his fear; he trembled because he imagined his children growing weaker, the helplessness he and Mathilde would feel, once they had given them all that was left and they'd be watching their decline without being able to do a thing, other than cut into their own flesh, the time it took for their own bodies to die, they would have eaten Blind Boy long ago by then, in his dreams, Corentin heard the shot from the rifle, killing the dog, and he woke in a sweat.

One year and eight months, there would be five of them by then, because Mathilde's belly was full and round once again, and once again it was madness, even worse than before, she said so herself in the evening. This is madness, the future can only get worse and worse.

Corentin recited the names of the stars, the ones he could remember, to find a name for the child to come.

Altair and Electra were one year old.

They turned blond, like Mathilde. They had never lost their pale skin, since the sun still encountered impenetrable layers of cloud and dust. But their cheeks turned pink from running around outside, and their eyes were blue like the sky no one had seen since the catastrophe.

Desert, silence, gray frozen nature. They didn't mind. They'd never known anything else. They didn't know what regrets were.

Corentin watched them, fascinated. He envied them their impossible carefree nature, their oblivion. Thus, nothing in this world was inscribed in genes, everything had to be learned all over again from the moment of every new birth. For Altair and for Electra, the lunar landscape they were growing up in was normal. As was the absence of comfort, of sunshine, of other people. And the fact that there was only one dog, and that his eyes were white. And the insipid, monotonous contents of the cans that made up their diet; the emptiness of the countryside; how very long the night lasted. The light that never really came completely, the cold that never really let them go.

They listened to Corentin telling stories of hares, foxes, silvery fish. Their gaze followed his slow gestures as he reminisced about the tall forests, the fruit trees at the end of the garden, basketfuls of little golden plums, and Augustine would make huge pies, and the smell of the dough baking into a crust, and the taste of cider, afterwards, when the pies had cooled.

The twins probably didn't understand much of what Corentin was saying, as he stared into the distance, his eyes focused on the images in his memory, the wonders he spoke of as if in a dream—and Corentin probably also couldn't understand what they had in their heads and were trying to say when it was their turn to babble. But there were voices: the father's when he went deep into his soul for the memory of times of joy, and which vibrated with recollections, trembled with illusory delight; and the little children's, even though they didn't know how to speak yet, just chirped from one sound to the next, believing they were making words, jubilant and happy words which everyone could grasp and make their own. At moments like this, they were together. You could tell from the smiles, the excitement in the phrasing, the cries. You could tell from the electricity in the air, charged with the things passing between them: Corentin often held out his arms and the children rushed into his embrace. It was such a deep emotion—this impression that his heart was melting, burning, exploding. Afterwards he was always astonished to find that with so much love and radiant warmth the world had not reverted to its former enchantment.

* * *

At the end of the month of July, Mathilde began to worry. She was nearing term, give or take a few weeks, since she had no exact points of reference. In reality, she knew nothing—neither the date, nor whether it was a boy or a girl, nor whether it was alone or accompanied yet again. It didn't really matter: it's just that she was apprehensive. Remembering the twins' birth. This time, Augustine wouldn't be there.

And deep down, it was terribly important. She wanted the birth to go well, she had children to raise and to love.

But Augustine wasn't there anymore.

Of course, there was Corentin, and Altair, and Electra. But she mustn't expect anything from them on that day.

She kept telling herself this to get used to it. She'd have to manage on her own.

She told Corentin, so her voice would say it, so it would exist.

You'll take care of the little ones. I'll manage the rest.

She looked out the window. Outside, the children were still playing—she looked in their direction, didn't see them. Her thoughts were elsewhere. She was thinking about death. She wasn't doing it on purpose, and it wasn't a premonition. It just came. Maybe because of the previous time, when without Augustine—Augustine wasn't there anymore.

Mathilde looked out the window. Her blue eyes were as gray as the sky. She couldn't see the twins, but she knew they were there, just behind, in the garden.

She had to stay alive for them. She would have to force out the little creature in her belly, and save everything—herself, and it, and them.

The first time she hadn't been thinking about anything. Women had been bringing children into the world forever—she herself already had. It was so normal. So ordinary.

So dangerous.

How many children this time? One, two, three? All at once.

How many hours, how many screams. Of course, she was afraid.

* * *

When it came, it was evening. She got up, her face ashen, and Corentin immediately understood. The last few days they'd hung curtains here and there to give the big bed some privacy. The twins slept at the other end of the room. Mathilde's first thought was for them—that with the heavy sleep of childhood they wouldn't hear. Her second thought, for the child to come: make it quick. Please.

Corentin was with her. Mathilde smiled at him, squeezed his hand. Suddenly she was grateful to him for being there.

Well. Let's try to do better.

He brought towels and water. She stretched out and gazed at the spider's webs on the ceiling. Before, she would have told herself she had to get rid of them, she'd been neglectful; but now, she studied the patterns, the woven threads, the silken design. It was pretty. It was light. Suddenly the pain was there, as if a giant were banging inside her belly to get out. She wanted to ask Corentin, when will it be over? The way children ask, when they've only just sat down in the car—are we there yet. But no one knew, Corentin no more than she did. One second at a time, she thought. The first sweat filled her with anxiety. It all came back in a flash. It was both so long ago and so recent. Barely more than a year. It all came back, the pain, the blood, the exhaustion beyond anything within reason. Augustine's hands on her, in her, bringing out the babies—all the more so because she, Mathilde, couldn't take it anymore, she had given up, she remembered. Her body stiffened. It wasn't contractions, but fear. She had to relax, not to make things worse. Corentin caught a glimpse of her wan smile. She gave a wave of apology.

She really had to relax.

To trust in—who, what?

Inside, she could feel the kicking. She thought: a little boy.

And then: it's not the same pain as last time.

It will be all right.

That was Corentin murmuring. For her, for him. She nodded her head, giving him an intense gaze. In spite of everything they were trying to make themselves believe, the suffering was beginning. The labor, the midwives called it.

Mathilde squeezed her hands over the sheets.

It's going to take a long time.

She didn't want to scream, because of the sleeping children. And yet she did scream. She bit into a cloth so it wouldn't be so loud. She stifled her cries, transformed them into spasms, terrified bouts of trembling. Bit by bit, she acknowledged the pain. Drowned it in Corentin's whispers as he bent over her, although she didn't know if it was really him, or if Augustine had come back.

She stared so hard at the spider's webs on the ceiling it was unsettling.

I have to make it.

And in her mind, she said, like a mantra: come on, come on, come on.

At one point she lost all awareness of time. All that remained was this body of hers, under attack. She felt as if some other creature were lifting it up, wringing her out, twisting her in every direction.

Please.

Until on August 27, before dawn, or at least that's what she thought, Sirius was born.

* * *

Was it because Corentin had kept in the habit of walking through the garden every morning to murmur a few words on Augustine's grave that he saw them?

Was it because he was walking slowly, and because, at that particular moment, he'd stopped looking at the sky?

Was it, as he'd believe with all his strength, because there was still a little enchantment in the world, enough to give them a gift, perform an impossible trick, was it for them in the end, because they'd stood fast, hadn't given up, hadn't thrown in the towel?

The plants had sprouted in a few days. They were scattered,

like unruly little green soldiers, spread haphazardly around the garden. Their leaves had pushed back the ashen earth but were scarcely open. They rose barely an inch above the ground. Corentin recognized them at once.

Augustine had always grown potatoes. Red ones, with pale flesh so firm they would keep nearly a year. They had burned in the catastrophe, the roots had shriveled and rotted—everything had vanished.

What had remained—probably crushed, stinking pieces of old tubers—had been scattered by Altair and Electra as they played; taken from the ground, put back with a laugh. And yet, there had been something left. Something had begun to quiver, waiting perhaps for this very event, to be found, exhumed—and with a little magic in their hands, someone would order it to live again.

Corentin put a hand on his chest, his heart was racing, the words he wanted to say would not come out. He slowly made little mounds around each plant, stroking the earth, not daring to do more for fear of spoiling everything. The green leaves carpeting the vegetable garden were like a miracle. All around there was not a single blade of grass, not one bud on a tree.

A mirage.

But Corentin stroked them—they really were there.

When he got back, he checked the date in his notebook. September 6.

So, spring had come, here it was.

Corentin had been waiting for two years: here it was.

He began to laugh and to weep.

On September 19, Blind Boy, who'd been missing for two days, came back. But he wasn't alone.

Corentin had already noticed that something was changing. Ten days earlier, just after Sirius was born, he'd heard the sound at night. And maybe he should have been glad that there were other creatures still alive somewhere nearby, moving around imperceptibly and silently, whose presence he could only guess at from the strange singing that made his blood run cold. But it was something he could not possibly be glad of.

These were not the creatures he'd hoped to find in the countryside.

Deep in the darkness an ancient fear rose from his gut, an unfamiliar fear, which only his genes had identified. It took him several minutes to put a name to it.

Several minutes to listen through the door.

To open it ever so cautiously and tell Blind Boy to come in—but once again Blind Boy wasn't there, and Corentin's fear increased.

In the distance, the singing had started up again. Thinking about it, Corentin would realize he should have noticed, there had been so many little signs, it hadn't just started a day or two ago, or even ten, but weeks ago, perhaps months—it was their nature to stay invisible, and by the time you heard them, it meant they were already somewhere very near.

Corentin closed the door, locked it, leaned back against the wood. He brought an armchair up to block it. It was useless, a futile instinct. There were windows with broken panes or poorly fixed bits of wood to replace them. There were too many ways to get in, if they wanted to.

But they wouldn't get in. They would wait outside.

He listened closely one more time, to be sure.

He was sure.

They meant the return of the ancient times.

Wolves.

* * *

Blind Boy showed up again on September 19, just when Corentin had accepted the fact he'd never see him again. The wolves' howling was too close, and there were too many of them. They weren't afraid of humans, let alone of dogs. They must be dying of hunger. They were coming closer, probably one night at a time; that morning the children were not allowed to play in the garden. With their brows pressed against the last remaining windowpanes in the living room, they listened. They imitated.

Ah-woooh.

They didn't laugh. This was indeed a language they were trying to establish, an answer, other words. Corentin had reinforced the doors and windows with big wooden planks hastily nailed in place. He knew that they'd be safe inside. But it had to hold. After that, the wind could blow, the wolves could huff and puff.

It was like something out of a bad fairy tale. Only in fairy tales did wolves huff and puff. In reality, all they had to do was wait, while they sat around the house.

Corentin counted his remaining ammunition and readied his rifle. He could kill a large pack. The first one. Not the one that would follow—because others would follow.

At one point, Altair reached for the door handle. It was only an effort, an intention, because the handle was too high. But he wanted to open the door. He wanted to go and see them. Mathilde had screamed.

Since then, they always kept the door locked.

And that day, Blind Boy came back, and he wasn't alone.

* * *

He had six puppies running after him, clumsy and unruly.

At that very moment, Corentin was certain the wolves had been there much longer than he realized.

And she—she stayed back, at the edge of what had been the forest. Her coat was barely visible against the gray, rain-washed bark of the trees.

Corentin didn't open the door.

He watched her, his eyes open wide.

Blind Boy was at the door now, looking at him—was he looking?—through the window.

Corentin looked at down at the puppies.

Wolfdogs.

What do you want? he said.

So Blind Boy rose up on his hind legs, facing him, pressing against the door. He was several inches taller than Corentin. It was like looking into a strange mirror, a mirror that reflected another creature, gigantic, just there on the other side of the glass—the glass began to quiver, the wood creaked. Corentin stepped back, stretched out his arm to hold the door.

The dog slowly dropped down and looked behind him.

The she-wolf wasn't moving. Wasn't coming any closer.

Mathilde and the children had clustered around Corentin; the twins were calling out to Blind Boy, confused, joyful exclamations, reaching their hands out to the puppies.

He's come for food, said Corentin.

He's come for refuge, said Mathilde.

And it was the same thing.

It was impossible.

Like everything that had been impossible since the catastrophe: it happened.

* * *

In the days that followed, Corentin worked hard to build a wooden stockade around the garden and the house. He also created a large pen—if they had to lock up the dogs, if they stayed, if there weren't any sudden changes.

The entire time he was outside he never took his eyes off the forest; sometimes a lament or a cry could be heard.

The wolves were there.

The she-wolf hadn't moved from the edge of the woods.

Blind Boy stayed close to Corentin. On guard. He had two bite-marks on his spine that Corentin hadn't noticed before, but they weren't oozing. The dog listened, his ears constantly flicking. His body, motionless.

The puppies, inside with Altair and Electra, were playing, sleeping, running. Mathilde had put Sirius's cradle in a safe place.

The puppies ate.

Pancakes of flour and water, leftover gruel or soup when there was some. Corentin and Mathilde refused to give them more than that. Sometimes all six of them would disappear into the woods. Maybe the she-wolf still had some milk.

One of the puppies was blind.

So, Corentin reckoned, it wasn't the catastrophe. It was a defect, a genetic trace.

The twins would wait by the door, whining with impatience. When the puppies came back, there was a mutual display of jubilation, then they fell asleep together on the carpet.

Corentin didn't know what Mathilde must be thinking when she gazed at them silently.

Corentin himself wondered if they could eat the dogs when they got bigger. And initially the thought of it sickened him, and he rejected it. Then he gave it some more thought. Of course, it was possible. It was simply returning what had been given, and he looked at them and thought they were too small and too thin.

But they mustn't feed them, mustn't waste their supplies.

And clearly the wolves had found their own means to survive, because the she-wolf was still there, and Blind Boy didn't eat much, then he would go off, yet he stayed big and solid.

If he'd been sure, Corentin would have gone to have a look in the woods, too.

To see whether some wildlife had returned—but where from? And feeding on what—old roots, hard wood, earth and pebbles.

If he could have been sure the wolves were gone.

He'd never seen the others, only the mother at the edge of the forest, but he didn't trust his eyes or his ears.

Maybe there was something to eat out there.

Would Blind Boy realize if he killed a puppy to cook it? Could he bring himself to do it? Yes, absolutely, for his children, that he was sure of.

The wondering was driving him crazy, though, along with time that would neither pass quickly nor fatten up the too-young wolfdogs.

* * *

He knew their exact number: eighty-seven potato plants. The leaves had grown, he had hilled the earth, had watched the sky and the pallor of the sun they could still just make out somewhere behind the layers of mist. He and Mathilde had reinforced the fences to protect the garden. They didn't water, the rain came often enough, they hoped it wasn't acidic anymore.

The seedlings grew. Not quickly, not robustly. Stunted little seedlings, and Corentin often thought that when time came to harvest them, maybe there would be nothing at the end of these timid roots, these flowers that would not bloom, nothing but crushed hope and empty peels.

He thought about potatoes, about their smell, if someday Mathilde did manage to grill them in a pan, or if they cooked them in the fireplace, wrapped in aluminum foil. In the early days, they'd had some he'd brought back from the gutted stores in the Little Town, but for over a year now—his mouth watered at the thought, his stomach rumbled, and he prayed that the seedlings would be fertile.

There were times he would gaze at them, hoping with nothing more than the strength of his conviction to give them vigor; at other times he would turn his back on them for fear that— he didn't know what, exactly, the same thing as when people say a watched kettle never boils. It was the first thing he did every day, just before lighting the wood stove: a quick glance out the window, as if the night might have pulled up the seedlings, as if something might have gotten in and wrecked everything. But nothing happened, nothing changed.

Not even the flowers, which had grown a little but did not open completely, wilted little white buds, and a few leaves beginning to turn yellow in places.

And so, one November morning, Corentin dug up a plant—to see. He marked a large perimeter with the spade, had trouble lifting the lump of earth, he thought he might replant it, if the tubers were too puny. He dug it up because the seasons didn't mean anything anymore and he was afraid of missing the right moment. He was afraid that if he waited any longer, they'd run the risk of a harvest of soft moldy potatoes, already spoiled. He held his breath. In this earth, lay their survival—or not.

Mathilde was there with Sirius in her arms. Corentin looked at her and she nodded. He put the spade in front of him and split the earth.

Go ahead.

He didn't expect them to be fine specimens, and they weren't. But there were potatoes. They weren't big; but—he counted them—there were twelve on the stem. He cried out.

Twelve!

He and Mathilde burst out laughing at the same time.

A nd it wasn't the beginning of a rebirth.
It wasn't the end of their fears.
The fears would remain, and the pain, and the difficulties of everyday life in a world that wasn't coming back to life.

They almost never saw the sun.

And it was just as well: because the one time it did emerge from the clouds, the only time it shone a fine yellow light, and they rushed outside, spinning around, arms spread wide—they turned and turned, and that evening, they had to tend their burns.

Because the ozone layer was gone, Corentin would think, the ozone layer had been damaged by the catastrophe and would take years, tens or thousands, to re-form. So, provided the sun didn't reappear . . . and it only reappeared once or twice, and Mathilde and Corentin kept the children inside.

Except on those rare occasions, it would be overcast forever.

And for those who had known something else, the monotony of the sky, the cool humidity that had become their daily lot, except for the three months of the year they could call summer when the air grew slightly warmer: this climate would slowly crush them, stifle them, remove all wonder and joy.

For five years, for ten years, they hoped the seasons would come back, they prayed for the return of springtime and warm weather, but it didn't come, or only so little.

All the same, Mathilde and Corentin could not help but look outside in the morning, like before, when there was often a surprise, when the weather was always changing; they had gotten into the habit as children, and depending on what they saw through the window, they would change their plans for the day, change their clothes, change their mood. But that was all over now. They saw their own children, who never looked outside when they got up and were getting dressed, because the weather was always the same, always gloomy, and there was nothing to see, no magic, no light, no change from the day before, or the day before that, or the eight hundred days that had gone before, then the thousand, and soon enough, three thousand.

They survived on Augustine's potatoes. Each time, Corentin kept a few more tubers to plant the following year, even though there was no following year, and he had realized he could plant them whenever he wanted, and everything grew all the same, every time—with the same mediocrity and regularity. The eighty-seven potato plants became two hundred, then three hundred, he put them into the earth every three or four months, and they ate them every day.

As the years went by, there was nothing else left, more or less. Corentin sometimes went back to the Little Town. Altair had turned five and showed unusual determination, and he would go with him, seeking out the slightest relic of food with the methodical single-mindedness of a bloodhound, opening every door of every cupboard in every remote spot, and often he would turn up a jar, a pot, or a can, and even though all the sell-by dates had expired by then, they were never sick.

They spread their net, a little farther, above all wider, to the isolated houses—a farm, a cabin, a hamlet with three or four buildings Corentin had never explored. And for all that the town had gradually been depleted by the successive raids of survivors, the places off the beaten track, which weren't visible from the road, the ones you had to know about to find—these places had escaped the plundering. Sometimes they returned with entire bags full of old food, and Mathilde wept with joy. But she didn't plan any feasts. She was sparing with everything. She would rather enhance their daily fare with a mouthful of sun-dried tomatoes, or a tablespoon of powdered soup, and make it last for weeks. No one found any reason to complain.

When Altair was ten, he asked to go beyond the circle Corentin had drawn on the map with its worn folds; he had circled their house with a gray line and pointed to the villages.

Here. And here.

Corentin shook his head. It would take all day. Or they would have to overnight along the way. It was a crazy idea.

But we've got Blind Boy to protect us, said the boy. And the rifle.

Corentin refused to leave Mathilde and the children for that long.

But they have dogs, too.

It's not enough.

And what if I go on my own, with Blind Boy.

That's crazy. Crazy.

Corentin leveled his gaze at the little warrior's clear blue eyes.

You heard me. No.

Mathilde came over, their last-born in her arms.

He's right.

The boy's expression lit up.

Me?

No. Him. Corentin.

She never said, Papa.

* * *

There were six children in Augustine's house now. Two

little girls had been born two years apart, Garnet and Urania. And finally, a little boy, Perseus, who was almost three.

And it was because of them that Corentin knew the catastrophe would be lasting, because of them that he hadn't completely lost track of time. He watched them grow, become bony and fragile, with that chalky skin he had grown used to, and their clear eyes that never saw the sun. They were lively, like the children from before. But they tired quickly, and that was different, and Corentin's heart sank, these children fed on starch and a few rare treats, which were always cause for celebration, children who would never grow taller than him, who would stay slight, and wiry, like Corentin himself had become.

And if they got sick, they would die; already twice—before Urania and after Perseus—Mathilde and Corentin had lost a child. For the space of a night or a week, their names had been Stella and Sham. Then something had come for them. Neither Mathilde nor Corentin would ever know what. Nor would they ever know whether the babies might have been saved—they figured they shouldn't even ponder it, but the question was there all the same, and it was awful to think that before, when there had been hospitals, Stella and Sham might have lived; awful to think that the world had regressed and couldn't get going in the right direction.

Sham had been the last child.

* * *

Mathilde held her empty belly, and her soul was like her flesh.

At night, close against her, Corentin finally fell asleep, exhausted.

Mathilde was also exhausted. But sleep would not come.

Maybe because, right up to the last minute, she had been holding the baby that didn't make it, and she could do nothing.

For four days, she'd kept him pressed against her skin to keep him warm, so that her heart would beat against his, and he'd find the rhythm, find the way to keep going. Sham—the baby didn't cry. He breathed slowly. Perhaps everything was normal, but Mathilde, overcome with anxiety, felt him leaving her. It went on for a day, then two, then three.

He stopped eating and she knew it was over.

And she'd wept, begged, cried out.

Sham died and she could do nothing.

Just loosened her hold when Corentin came to her and said so very gently, I'll bury him in the garden, next to Stella.

Yes, opening her arms had been the most painful thing. She could still feel the unspeakable wrenching; she'd closed her eyes in vain.

She went on getting up in the morning, speaking, singing for the others. There was that tiny grave in her head, which forced her to sit down from time to time, when the sorrow became too raw. Twice now; two graves. There would be no others. Mathilde did not want to give birth to dead children. She couldn't stand it. She was made for life, and something had faltered inside her, doubt had overcome her.

Do you understand?

That is what, weeks later, she murmured to Corentin when he placed his hand on her. When she said: It's over. But it wasn't Sham she was talking about. It was them. She'd made her decision. It wasn't a question, not even a request. That's the way it was. There would be no more children. There would be no more of Corentin's body on hers.

Do you understand?

They already had six children. Six children they struggled to feed, and no one knew what would happen to them ten or twenty years from then (or tomorrow), children growing like wild grasses, fragile and ephemeral, they had to take care of those children.

And it was already a huge thing to have had six babies in these ten years of torment, when they were sure of nothing, when every day brought into question everything they thought they had gained the day before, everything they had dreamt of for the future, because the future was no different from the present, it would not change, it would always be despair.

We're crazy, Mathilde murmured.

And she was right.

Crazy.

So Corentin had agreed, in a hushed voice. He had said, All right. He moved away in the bed and put one arm over Mathilde's belly, and after that, he didn't move.

A nd maybe that was his last chance.

Maybe Mathilde, by keeping her body from him, had just saved him.

When she began to explain, gently pushing him away with both hands, he thought he would get angry.

Mathilde too thought he would. He had seen it reflected in her eyes.

But the anger didn't come.

Something he hadn't expected: mere sorrow.

Corentin thought about these ten years gone by, and only sadness remained. His children loved him—his children who were his future, his only purpose, his joy. He'd managed to make sure they'd be fed with a field of potatoes that to him seemed immortal; the house was warm every morning; Blind Boy brought back new puppies for them to play with, to run and tumble.

Only sadness.

It was long, ten years of sorrow and—at first, he didn't understand why the thought came to him—ten years of solitude.

Was it because of her, Mathilde?

Mathilde, who didn't love him.

And they didn't deserve this, either one of them, the coldness between them, when life was already so difficult. And yet he was the one who'd wanted—who'd obliged Mathilde to repopulate the earth, in their small way, and he'd been right, of course, even Mathilde herself had experienced a sort of rebirth by bringing them into the world; but he'd known from the beginning that she wished it weren't him, she'd never over-come the glaring injustice of it, why had the others died, why did she have to make do with Corentin, it was pointless to even wonder, now, she had to look at these new children and tell herself that all the answers were to be found in them, that they would be all they needed.

That evening, when Mathilde told Corentin she didn't want to have any more little, dead children, that is what he was thinking.

Six children: maybe that was enough for the earth.

And if he changed, might Mathilde love him someday?

* * *

So Corentin began to look more closely at the six children and the seventeen dogs.

To look at Blind Boy, who was getting old, his flanks becoming hollow.

The she-wolf hadn't been there for two or three years—he hadn't written it down in his notebook, he just noticed one day that she was no longer there at the edge of the woods, and he didn't know how long it had been. Had she gone away, had she died? There were only her offspring now, fully-grown or still young; Corentin had built two large enclosures, one for the males, and one for the females, he'd had to separate them to pre-vent inbreeding. The nights during rutting period, or when the moon was full, they would howl like wolves, their cries piercing the darkness. The children liked those nights. The wolfdogs' howling lulled them; Mathilde gazed at their smiles as they slept.

What a strange world, she thought.

The wolves—the real ones—had gone away.

At one point, Corentin had killed a few, then skinned them

where the children couldn't see him. Mathilde had made stew. Cooked for a long time—a very long time—it wasn't that different from any other meat, something between pork and beef, stronger, gamier. You just mustn't think about it. It was meat, that was all. And maybe it was like dog meat, but they'd never eaten dog meat.

* * *

With every litter, there was a blind one.

With every litter, Corentin never managed to kill them so there would be fewer, because the she-wolf would not let them near the house until they were a few weeks old. And nature also took care of selection, because most often there were only three or four of them—in all likelihood the weakest ones had died or been devoured by the males, or abandoned by their mother, who knew they were unfit.

Seventeen dogs behind a stockade, and during the day, the children would let them out in groups of two or three, and run with them, and roll on the ground.

It was complicated finding food for seventeen dogs. Corentin was relieved when the she-wolf disappeared.

Many years before, in the Little Town, he'd made off with all the bags of kibble and cans of dog food—cat food too, it made no difference.

They'd eaten it, too, those strong-smelling pâtés that made them wrinkle their noses. But when you're hungry.

How far will we go, he wondered.

Will we become animals, too.

* * *

By the tenth year after the catastrophe, a few trees had come back to life.

Not the tall ones. Not the ones in the Forests.

But smaller ones, which didn't require as much to regenerate; he saw them one day as he was walking with Altair past a nursery in the outskirts of the Little Town. They dug up a few of them and took them home—fruit trees.

Most of them died the following year.

There were three left. One cherry plum and two apple trees.

Every morning, Corentin ran his hands over their smooth bark, trying to instill strength into their frail trunks.

He couldn't bear the thought that there were no more bees.

In this world, everything had mutated.

Everything was dead, but equally, everything was possible.

The fruit trees grew slowly. And although it was a lie, Corentin told himself it didn't matter. He had time.

In reality, he didn't have time. It was urgent. They needed the fruit for the children, to help their vitamin-deficient bodies that made do with too little. He placed all his hope in those three little trees, as he had in the potatoes, with fear and faith, he touched them, and it seemed to him he could feel the sap flowing behind the bark, it seemed to him he could hear the beating of their deep rhythm. When there wasn't enough rain, he would bring buckets of water from the stream with Altair and Sirius. After many long months, buds appeared, which gave birth to leaves that were stunted, but green and smooth, since there were no longer any parasites or diseases; what they needed was energy, the will to grow, and that was written in their genes, the temptation of life surpassing everything. He could see this in every creature that was still there—the children, the dogs, the rare insects, birds, and grasses he had seen these ten years.

There was weariness. There was failure, like the seeds that didn't sprout, or potato plants that withered, or the roof leak along the eaves that Corentin didn't know how to fix (all he did was roll bits of plastic into a ball and wedge them into the spots where the tiles were broken, to keep the water out). The night the chimney caught fire, and they threw sand and earth to douse it, plagued with fear that the shaft might be cracked and no longer fit for use. The days when snow prevented them from going out, burying the house under a white blanket six feet deep, and they always dug a tunnel to reach the outside. Corentin recalled those weeks of ice with a sort of wonder. The tunnel was like an elongated igloo—but the children didn't know what an igloo was. It was just a gallery, four or five yards long, dazzlingly white, with smooth walls that flashed with sparks whenever a little light crept in. It was like a magical space, an airlock leading from one world to another where anything could happen. They walked slowly down the tunnel, wishing it were endless. Their muffled murmurs resonated, their hands stroked the damp walls. There were places where the walls were thinner and more translucent, and they would gaze at the countryside through a frozen scrim, with the impression they were both in the world and elsewhere; they did not feel imprisoned, they believed they were safe.

When the snow melted and the tunnel disappeared, it took them several days to recover from the loss and shake the habit of that strange state of white, frozen consciousness when they opened the door; the little ones asked where the ice house had gone.

And they always went everywhere together, made every effort to survive together. They made up an inseparable whole.

And none of the children ever said that life wasn't worth living. The question did not exist. Survival kept them so busy. As did, equally, the force that unfailingly bound them together.

A nd the years went by, on and on.
They were still there.
Still six of them, with Mathilde and Corentin.
And there were dogs.

Blind Boy had died. Corentin chose a young blind dog from the pack and took him with him. He gave him the same name. A sort of continuity, he thought, and this reassured him, lessened the pain he'd felt on finding the big dog lifeless outside the door one morning; only Blind Boy had ever been free, day and night.

Because Altair and Electra, and Sirius, and Garnet, and Urania and Perseus had sometimes escaped their parents' attention and left the doors to the enclosures open, other dogs had been born. They seemed normal, so Corentin let them grow up.

The apple trees had made it. The plum tree died. There would be no more pies like the ones Augustine used to make.

They harvested little gray-green apples. When the fruit was ripening, Corentin would stare for a long time at the two young trees. Maybe they were a self-fertilizing species, maybe some incomprehensible arrangement with nature.

He missed the taste of meat. He'd forgotten how it used to smell, on the grill, just remembered how good it had been. He could share this memory with Mathilde alone, it made their eyes glow, made them shrug their thin shoulders.

The children didn't know what an ox or a duck was.

At first, Corentin had tried to explain it to them.

He'd made drawings.

But what was the point.

* * *

Eighteen years had gone by.

There was no need to say since. The catastrophe was the world's new ground zero.

Eighteen years, since the blast, the fire, the desolation. Eighteen years on the scale of humankind or the planet was nothing; but time had never seemed longer. Eighteen years that felt like a hundred or a thousand, when the hope of better days left them impatient, champing at the bit; when the only point of these days was to find a way to survive, to make it to the days to come—finding food, chopping firewood, praying that nothing worse would happen.

Eighteen years was an infinity. The age of Altair and Electra. Corentin felt so old. He looked at Mathilde, who was between forty and forty-five years old, like him; they no longer celebrated birthdays, they had nothing to celebrate with, no presents, no fine meals, the notion of a party was ludicrous.

Mathilde was still a beautiful woman. But like Corentin, she felt old. Hardship had worn them down; their hopes crushed one after the other were scattered through years that counted double. This was visible in the fine strands of silvered hair on their brows and temples; it could be felt in a new, imperceptible tiredness, less resistance, less strength to chop wood or carry the buckets from the stream, when the children had wandered off somewhere. There was lassitude, too, snatches of lassitude every day; after eighteen years, it weighed heavily on their shoulders.

* * *

Corentin would sit at the edge of the circle the six children made when they were talking, and he observed them. What he was gazing at in those moments, he knew, was the core of his existence. The only thing he could not survive if it were to die. Mathilde often joined them, sat down among them. Corentin could feel her shoulder against his. As crazy as it might seem, he wished these moments would never end. He would accept the end of the world for the rest of his life, as long as he had his children around him, and Mathilde's shoulder rubbing gently against his.

The children would go on talking and talking, they were voluble, they filled the air with their light voices, their little laughs, their teasing, and Corentin looked at Mathilde while she was looking at them.

* * *

And this vision of Mathilde was all tenderness and attentiveness. She loved them all, her children, all so similar: blond, slim (when they weren't downright skinny), pale. And all different, too.

Altair, his spirit, his fierce determination. Because he was the eldest; because he had been the first one to struggle to find his place, perhaps—Altair never gave up, never threw in the towel, either when it came to impossible tasks, or the craziest issues or ideas. Altair had climbed to the top of a tall, dead sequoia to fetch an incomprehensibly intact blue ribbon, more than 135 feet above the ground, more than 135 feet of dead branches cracking one after the other as he climbed. Because Urania had asked him to. Because she wanted to know if that scrap of blue was the moon their parents talked about, so Altair went to find out, despite Electra's screams.

Electra—she'd become a miniature Mathilde, and her mother would gaze at her and melt with happiness. A little girl, then not so little, who only liked others, only thought of others, only took care of others. She consoled, encouraged, helped; she was always there for them. She slipped over the world, light-footed, ethereal. Anywhere else they would have called her a ghost; she was a sort of fairy, the air burst with light as she went by, she was bathed in it, her voice sang with each word. Electra the Brave—that was what Mathilde called her, to herself; she recognized herself in her daughter, a strange mirror, a near-perfect reflection. First up, last to bed, Electra made it a point of honor to relieve her mother of the day's first chores—wood in the stove, food set out on the table that morning for breakfast.

Early on, they'd stopped having a meal at noon. They had a snack, a sort of make believe, as if. No meal: they had to save on their provisions. The babies had their bottle, the others would get a sort of gruel, a sludge, often bizarre, soggy mixtures. No one fussed. Mathilde remembered that before, in the place that had been India, most people had only one meal a day.

And so, they too, now—Mathilde had trouble saying the word in her head, it seemed so awful to her: they too didn't get enough to eat, either, they went *hungry*. Until the catastrophe, this was something that happened only in poor countries.

But they'd gotten used to it. Sometimes on cold or damp days, when they'd been cutting branches and trees for hours, Mathilde would come up with a surprise for them. They'd come home and it would smell of warm, sugary potatoes. After a while there was no more sugar, and then she would leave the spuds to get brown on the edges and they could almost imagine they tasted of caramel.

And then, once nature was on its way again, in fits and starts, they came upon some birch trees in the forest. Not much to look at, a birch tree. Not tall, let alone robust. But like all these scrawny little living things, a birch tree didn't need much to learn how to live again, far less than a centuries-old oak tree—no centuries-old oak or beech or fir tree had survived.

Corentin made holes in the bark with a hand drill then rammed in a piece of plastic for a spout. The sap ran out and they collected it in plastic bottles they attached to the trunk. The first time, the children brought their treasure back to Mathilde with cries of joy. Sirius ran the fastest. He was shouting.

Sugar, sugar.

Mathilde burst out laughing as she took the bottle from his hands. But it was true: even if they couldn't remember the taste of sugar, it smelled of sugar. Of molasses. Their potatoes became a celebration, and they were glad of the smallest thing.

Sirius had put his bottle on the table and gazed longingly at his mother until she congratulated him. Sirius had long blond curls—he wouldn't cut them, he liked it when the wind blew them into a wild tangle, he liked to tuck his curls behind his ears or tie them back the way the girls did; the day Mathilde forced him to cut his hair was a day of anger. He wanted to be like his sisters.

Garnet and Urania—they weren't twins, but they were inseparable. They weren't twins, but they were like two peas in a pod. Often, from a distance, Mathilde couldn't tell them apart. Two joyful little girls, two melancholy little girls. It was either one or the other. Depending on the day. They like to cuddle with their mother in the evening, with their big bluish eyes. They liked it when she told them stories.

It was tricky to come up with stories.

Tricky because they didn't know about anything.

When they were little and not yet asking too many questions, Mathilde would imagine a butterfly, an elephant, or a hen that made cakes.

But what was a butterfly, an elephant, a hen?

Corentin got involved. He drew pictures. They didn't

always understand—what was it for, how did it work. He would say, it's like Blind Boy, but it has a different shape.

No, it doesn't bark.

No, it doesn't fetch the pieces of wood you throw.

It was so hard.

Later, Mathilde would invent horses, boats, oceans, and the same thing happened. All the stories could only take place in a destroyed world, with people who looked like her children, and animals that were all called Blind Boy. The little girls could only identify themselves with what they saw. And even though Mathilde had found a few picture books, it meant nothing, seeing them flat on the paper, it didn't give them a shape or an existence, none of them would ever happen upon any of them outside—no horses, or boats, or oceans, it all felt like a falsehood.

And the sisters would applaud the poor stories and laugh, and their brothers would lean on their elbows next to them.

Afterwards, Perseus would ask a ton of questions. So many questions. He ought to be in school, thought Mathilde, ruefully. Books. Words. Causes for wonder, and sometimes, answers. The little boy talked non-stop. Even Electra, from time to time, would silence him with an exhausted gesture.

A little boy whose beauty was timid and striking. Mathilde sometimes said, With his doe eyes, with his feline movements, and only Corentin could understand. Only Corentin had the images in his mind.

The six of them made up Mathilde's world. Through them, she found the strength to go on, to wrench from the world the wherewithal to survive. It was too little, yet it sufficed.

Sometimes, from the top of the valley, Corentin would gaze at the world around him and look for signs of renewal. But they were infinitesimal. A few blades of grass here and there, growing through cracks in the pavement; a few leaves on a few trees. The forest remained black and empty, the tall figures of burned oaks and beech trees were still barren. Branches had broken over the years and lay scattered on the ground; they would use them for firewood, it was easier than felling tall trunks with axes. You could see through the forest: there were no lianas or ivy, no brambles to block your gaze. The earth was yellow, gray, black. And friable: the children brushed it with their feet as they ran, and clouds of dust rose up around them and made them cough.

You couldn't exactly say there was nothing in this world, because there were things. They were almost invisible, but Corentin could make out traces, clumps of earth that had been scratched at, little droppings that could only come from mammals or, perhaps, birds or bats. And yet, he couldn't hear anything in the branches, no birdsong or chirping, nothing in the forest, where there were no more leaves to tread on, nor the sound of footsteps, and it drove him crazy, because he knew they were there, somewhere. Perhaps they were peaceful, elusive animals—and perhaps they were predators lying in wait, so Mathilde and Corentin refused to let the children go far, refused to let them go alone, without a parent, or one of the dogs; they couldn't stop thinking about the wolves.

* * *

Corentin had seen some creatures return to the stream below: some sort of transparent larvae the size of a knuckle that didn't look like anything he had ever seen. He hadn't dared to catch one, hadn't dared try to eat one. They looked pre-historical to him, not fully formed, unfinished—mutant creatures, and who knew what was inside them, what radiation, bacteria, hidden disease.

So this is it, he thought, the world eighteen years after. And it was both a huge lapse of time and such a short period that it was normal nothing had yet had time to adapt or re-appear, it was beginning with the smallest creatures, insects, worms. How many years would it take for the universe to be a welcoming place again—Corentin could feel no resurgence of joy or well-being, he remained silent, it was his business; his sons and daughters, once again, did not miss the world from before. Only Mathilde's eyes would shine when he told her, on coming back from a walk with Blind Boy Number Three, that he'd found a shrew's burrow.

* * *

They had seen other human beings alive.

Four times since the twins were born. Four and a half times—the half time was when Corentin had caught a glimpse, so fleetingly that he couldn't swear there really had been human beings where he had looked a few seconds earlier, because in the time it took him to frown and adjust his vision, they had vanished. The image would haunt him for a long time, however, because they were the first living people he had seen in years. And the image would also stay in his memory because they gave him such a strange impression, a father and his son—or maybe, simply, it was a man and a child—pushing a shopping cart, and the shopping cart contained all their belongings, all their treasures. Corentin knew they had seen him. From a distance, he could make out the sudden hunch of their backs, the way they crouched in vain to hide, they left the road at once, and hid the shopping cart behind a gray clump of bushes. All movement had stopped. Corentin hesitated to go after them, to try and speak with them. But then, if they were so eager to hide . . . Was it fear, was it madness—he turned back and continued on his way, after giving a wave of his hand, and waiting for only a few seconds, he left.

The other times—the first three ones, it was also on the road.

With Altair and the second Blind Boy. And the third time with Sirius.

Dazed, exhausted survivors.

And afterwards Corentin turned to his sons and saw how fine and healthy they were compared to the creatures they had just seen, who looked like the scarecrows people used to put in the fields when he was young, when there was something to be harvested. Creatures so thin and haggard that Altair and Corentin would wonder, the first time, how they could go on standing upright on their legs, which weren't legs anymore, but two little sticks too frail to carry their bodies, even though they were so light and emaciated, two little bones with hardly any flesh, struggling to move forward, since everything else was still working—just barely. Right down to their depleted lungs, which left their voices so thin, so low that you had to listen carefully to hear them, and Corentin felt both powerful and guilty, he hadn't offered them anything, neither food nor help, they needed all they had.

The second time with Altair, the survivors were such sad ghosts, so dirty and repulsive, that he had shouted at them to come no closer. He feared disease more than anything. With no more contact with other human beings, their bodies didn't know how to defend themselves anymore. All their energy went into surviving—there was nothing left over. Maybe the group heading toward them would have insisted, but Blind Boy—his size, his growling that caused the air to tremble—Blind Boy had discouraged them. They stood facing each other for a long time, the ghost-like people on one side, Corentin and Altair and the dog on the other, separated by a mere nothing, an invisible border suddenly decreed by Corentin's shouts, and it kept them motionless on either side, within earshot; but they only exchanged a few words. Where were they, and Corentin told them the name of the Little Town, they looked on a map so worn it tore in their hands. Who were they—they didn't answer, they went on their way.

Who they were meant nothing anymore. And Corentin himself, if they'd asked him, what could he say. Saying his family name didn't matter anymore, neither did his profession, if he'd had time to have one. Belonging to the village—that was useless. His connection with Augustine and the Forests—but who knew Augustine, and who knew the Forests?

The third time, with his two eldest boys, Corentin had seen a group of women. Five gray, bowed figures, weary, gaunt creatures, shapeless beneath their layers of stinking threadbare clothing. And Sirius, his eyes open wide, had murmured, What are they?

The fourth and last time they encountered any humans—the fourth time was long after that.

T he routine of days, weeks and years was numbing. To liven up the monotony, they had no one but themselves: human beings and dogs.

Sometimes Corentin would watch his children playing. With nothing: sticks, damp earth, an old rag rolled into a ball they could throw or kick around. Sometimes they would just run after each other; other times they would argue. They dug steps into the trunks of dead trees in order to climb a little higher above the ground; they would alter the course of the stream by building a dam, which never lasted for long; they would map out winding paths to run along. The eldest, almost grown, went on playing as they always had with the younger ones, and sometimes sat down with them to tell stories.

Corentin always expected one of them would come crying to him and say, I'm bored. I don't know what to do.

How often had he said it to Augustine, who would roll her eyes and make a list of all the chores still to be done—the garden, the housework, the laundry, the firewood, tidying; was he sure he had nothing to do, because she could find him plenty to do, for sure.

Boredom. What incredibly good fortune, she would add. Boredom doesn't make your arms hurt, or your legs, or your back, or your hands, which had started to be distorted with arthritis. Boredom didn't buckle your body, make your mind go frantic. It was a blessed time: a time when you could invent the world. Nothing stopping you. Nothing forbidding you.

Corentin now knew that Augustine had been right. Thirty or thirty-five years ago, he had begun imagining, conceiving, creating, building. Stories, follies, castles in the sand or in images. He had understood infinity, and infinity was inside him. He was infinity.

That's what he could tell them.

But he didn't need to.

He never explained to them that boredom was an explosion, a burst of flames, because the children were never bored. They had glimpsed the exaltation of imagination, their capacity to make a world that existed only in their minds, and yet, for all that, it was the mind that gave it life. Corentin could see it reflected deep in their eyes, in fugitive images. It shone, it was yellow and orange and warm. He asked them to describe it to him. It didn't look like anything he'd ever known. He was tempted to tell them—it doesn't work that way, it doesn't exist, it won't exist, it's not possible.

But was it any more impossible than the world which had burned, and which was only just coming back to life?

They made things up without the knowledge of anything from before, starting with something new, with what their virgin minds could combine, suppose, imagine. It was both ridiculous and sublime. Corentin often raised his eyebrows, puzzled. The children's world led to questions he'd never asked himself. He spent hours with them: the older ones had their ideas for building things, they drew lines on the ground or sometimes on paper; the younger ones scribbled, added irregular lines or circles, their voices all raised together with dozens or hundreds of absurd and stunning ideas. Corentin didn't say much, he didn't want to interfere, to skew their thoughts, so totally free. He questioned; he listened. It reminded him—it was long ago, and took a very different form, but was so similar in its mad enthusiasm and absence of limits—of the epic nights in the catacombs. There were the same creative outbursts, the same feverishness, the same laughter. It never went anywhere, because one of the younger children would always end up trampling on the ground or on their papers, but no one shouted in protest, that's the way it was, the world would always be there to be remade, reinvented. Destruction left the door open to reconstruction. It left days and years to come.

* * *

Every morning, Corentin counted the children. Counted as their feet came down the stairs and ran over the tiles. As if they might have disappeared during the night. As if something could have captured them. Now all six of them slept in the attic—they wanted to make it their world, Mathilde and Corentin had agreed, and then they no longer had the right to go upstairs. Corentin, however, had insisted on installing an inner staircase through a trap door; he would not have the little children going outside—in the dark, if they'd had a nightmare, if the wolves. And then, it was warm. The soft air from the wood stove rose through the hearth space. Gone were the memories of nights so cold that even lying right up against the chimney shaft could not still the shivering.

The children had occasionally invited Mathilde and Corentin to visit their domain. The door to the attic opened onto something impossible and magical. They had hung colored sheets and pieces of cloth on the walls, from the ceiling, transforming the big bare room into a huge colorful tent, a labyrinth of cotton, wool, and things transformed into treasures—pieces of sculpted wood, pebbles sparkling with quartz, strange piles of things. They'd fashioned their own low sofas, stacking pieces of carpet with red and orange cushions; they'd designed a sort of cocoon to which they alone had the codes.

They put up boards at chest height to separate two sleeping areas, without closing them off altogether. The boys had settled on one side, the girls at the other end. In the middle, in this space where everything looked a mess yet had its place, there was something that was like nothing else, a disconcerting, yet, on closer inspection, abnormally joyful jumble. Something bordering on happiness.

E ighteen immense years.
   When the spring, for the first time, brought some color to the branches of certain trees, inventing a shower of green leaves in the middle of the black forest, Mathilde and Corentin had this stupid thought.

That life had regained the upper hand—life had started up again at last.

As the years went by, they would understand that this wasn't altogether true. It wasn't complete. Here or there, there might be a tree—the birch trees where they extracted their sweet sap; a few offshoots from a chestnut tree that would never yield any fruit: twisted little charms. There would be the odd clump of grass, or a little plankton in the stream. But everywhere else, all around, was gray, scraped earth, and nothing more.

But hope didn't need much to go on.

Everything's coming back, they murmured, gazing out at the desolate landscape.

And to be ready—what insane thought process made them imagine they had to be ready for this new world—they put twice the eagerness into accomplishing their daily chores, relentlessly planting, ensuring their dreary daily subsistence, reinforcing their ramshackle little buildings; and above all, they taught the children how to read and write.

* * *

It's for after, said Mathilde.

After what, she didn't say, either.

For years, she'd been showing them words, numbers, arithmetic; the globe which could no longer represent any sort of reality; but there, too, Mathilde made believe, she couldn't teach them an empty world.

With the older children she went as far as fractions, square roots, and the equations she remembered, $(a+b)^2 = a^2 + 2ab + b^2$, and it was surely pointless, but she explained all the same, along with the solution of unknowns, and everything that had gone to make up her old store of knowledge from school, and which she had never used, with chalk on a big slab of wood she showed them, talked to them about the United States, and Russia, and China, and she looked at them, and listened to them, and they knew so little.

And it was so unimportant.

What was important was that they were there.

Still alive.

In the course of those eighteen years, at one time or another, they had all been sick.

They had always recovered, through some miracle, Mathilde thought, because what if they had needed an operation, if there had been an emergency . . . Sirius had had a strange fever for weeks, and Urania had vomited so much that she'd lost nearly twenty pounds when she was ten years old, she'd become a little ghost who went on smiling as she faded away, watching her brothers and sisters running around the garden, and Mathilde wept in silence as she watched her from the kitchen, because there was nothing else she could do, because she didn't want to miss even a moment of her little girl's final days.

And then, like the leaves on the trees: it happened again.

Every time, it was a miracle.

Sirius woke up one morning and the fever was gone. Urania started eating again and her cheeks flushed with color.

Mathilde knew, she could feel it deep in her guts: the fear of seeing her children die had eaten away at her during those years, had worn down her soul and her body. But there was no room for tiredness or discouragement, no room for weeping or lamentation. She had to fight, all the time. That was their fate now. Soul-searching was a luxury that no longer existed. When you have to survive, you find unimagined inner resources, impossible strength. When you have to survive, you don't stumble: you don't fall until the last moment. And then it's for good.

Before, it was—Mathilde had forgotten what it was like, before.

Easy?

She didn't know anymore.

And yet, now, you couldn't rule it out, happiness. It could be found in these six children, some of whom were already young adults—the others were gradually getting there. Watching them grow up. Hearing them sing, when they were in the mood, and their voices echoed down the valley, rose into the gray sky. In the beginning, she'd forbidden them from singing. She was afraid they might be heard. But since no one ever went that way anymore. So, she listened to them, the songs she'd taught them, the songs that existed only in her memory, which had been erased from the world, songs about rainbows, and imagining, and yellow submarines, and Hallelujah. Their songs would float in the air, so incongruously, so inappropriately. And so joyfully.

Because the children—these children, they couldn't help it: they were joyful. It was nothing they did on purpose. It was in their nature. Even Altair and Electra, the eldest, who had outgrown the age of insouciance—even them. Before, they would have been serious. They would have had their plans for the future, and pressure, and responsibility, and anxiety. Was it really such a terrible place, this world where they could remain light-hearted and futile, where the littlest things filled them with wonder? Was that not a form of joy?

And Mathilde could not help but be thoroughly aware that she was lying to herself, that there could be no happiness deep down—the only reason there was happiness was because the six of them knew nothing else.

Like those birds that are raised alone and don't know they can chirp. Their ignorance was bliss. They were joyful because they lived in deceit.

They were fooled.

Pathetic, she thought, on the verge of tears, when her morale was low.

And yet, the questions arose, creative and embarrassing.

The three eldest—they had surges of feeling, impulses, urges, that no one could satisfy, their brothers and sisters were not enough, their world was too small. Mathilde took them to one side, explained, in a quiet voice, stroked their hair.

She knew the solution, contained in one word: leave.

But the thought of leaving was terrifying. Would they have the courage to abandon the little they had managed to re-create? Corentin thought about it every night from the moment Mathilde had told him: we have to leave.

For the children.

And something inside him just couldn't. He still believed the world would be repopulated, he was convinced that one day he would no longer be able to walk through the woods with Blind Boy without coming upon other people. Every sign—a blade of grass, a new tree, an insect that looked something like a bee—launched an absurd hope. And yet he knew it was impossible. No one had reappeared. No one had moved into the abandoned houses further up, none of the villages had been colonized. In the Little Town where Corentin, Altair, and

Sirius still roamed on occasion, they had never found a single trace of human presence.

They acted as if.

It was normal.

It was viable.

They didn't see the dead earth. It was their earth.

They didn't see the burned trees. The trees had always been like that.

They didn't see the dead stream—there were things in the stream, since the world was starting up again, the world was returning to life, cried Corentin. And it was Perseus who came back up from the stream one afternoon at a run, shouting to tell them the news.

There are creatures!

What sort of creatures—he didn't know how to explain, he didn't know what scales were, they were shiny, that was all. They went down, all eight of them.

Oh.

Corentin stopped them at water's edge, holding out his arm. He turned to Mathilde—she alone could understand.

Fish.

Fish?

Which looked nothing like the bleaks or the gudgeons they used to catch in the old days. Hybrids, mutants, almost transparent.

Fish. I'll be damned.

Can we eat them?

They caught two of them. With a net, because they had no fishing rods or worms.

The others got away.

Two little fish, as long as an open hand, skinny, full of bones. The children didn't like the smell, and Mathilde made a mince, mixing the grilled flesh with thick mashed potatoes. And then they said it was good, and Corentin looked at Mathilde.

They've come back.

She nodded, frowning. She knew what he would say next.

Maybe we can stay. Maybe everything will come back here—and Mathilde shook her head.

Apples, potatoes, and fish. And you think that's life? For you, for our children?

Don't say that.

I'm just saying it like it is.

T he fourth and last time they met any living people was at the end of the eighteenth year.

At home.

It was the first thing Mathilde thought when she saw them: they're here, at our home.

With the children—because of them.

The children had gone for a walk. All six of them. Mathilde had found it very difficult to agree to them going off on their own. For a long time, she kept the youngest ones at home, it troubled her, but this is what she thought: if anything happens to them, there will still be one, or two, or three. But as the little ones grew older, they wanted to go with their siblings, and she'd had to resign herself to letting them go—otherwise, she would have had to forbid all of them from going, and life was already so dull and routine.

They took dogs with them, chose them from the pen.

They weren't allowed to go beyond the first valley and the first hill, which was how far the dogs' barking could still be heard, and where Mathilde thought Corentin would have time to run if anything bad happened.

And when she was alone at the stove, during these strange moments of solitude while the children were roaming around the forest, Mathilde reproached herself for being anxious, and for the way she warned them every time—if they met any men, if they came upon an animal, if they had a bad feeling. She conveyed her fear to them, they didn't say anything, but she could see they were blocking their ears, making an effort not to hear. Altair and Electra were adults, the dogs were fierce, there was no one left anywhere to threaten them. And yet, that panic she felt on seeing them go off.

Hadn't she been right then, all these years.

Now, on this day, when a group of nine living humans were standing in the courtyard, and they weren't her children.

Not just that.

The children: they were the ones who'd brought the people back here. It was one scenario Mathilde had never imagined. She'd never dreamed they could be so thoughtless as to reveal their shelter and their hiding place to strangers: what had these people said to induce them to bring them here—what sort of ordeal had they threatened them with?

Nothing.

In the courtyard, talking in a lively fashion, laughing a little, even.

The children had brought these human beings here of their own free will.

On purpose.

But didn't I tell them? exclaimed Mathilde, putting down her kitchen towel. She saw Corentin from behind: he'd gone out, carrying the rifle.

When they saw him, they all raised their hands in a sign of peace, of submission. The two children with them also raised their arms.

* * *

Corentin looked at them. The adults, but above all the children—it was the first time he'd seen any in eighteen years.

These children, like his own: born after the catastrophe, thanks to who knew what terrifying life force, when everything was destroyed, and yet in spite of everything the world was being called on—obliged, compelled—to make a future. Children, like his own—thin and pale, their eyes too big for their faces, looking too exhausted for their age, children without a childhood, searching for a meaning to their presence here beyond fear and their parents' selfishness, beyond a primary instinct for which there was no longer any excuse: now they needed the proof that they'd been right to be born.

Corentin lowered the rifle. Blind Boy growled. In the pen behind them, the dogs were barking; they'd smelled something strange and new.

We're hungry, said the adults.

And it wasn't a demand, it wasn't a threat. It was a prayer, or an excuse, the kind you make when you have no strength for anything else, no resources left inside. An entreaty, it was in their eyes, and Corentin, terrified, thought that there were too many of them, that every tiny bit of food he might give them would not be enough, would be the food his own children would not get, tomorrow, or a year from now, and he looked with fury at Altair, Electra, and Sirius, and Garnet, and Urania, and Perseus, who had broken every rule of caution, carried away by who knew what stupid enthusiasm, staggering naïveté, who had shown the way to these starving humans, to people he didn't want here and who frightened him.

And now his children were clapping their hands, shouting with joy, appealing to their father and mother, begging them, too—can we give them something to eat, can they stay, can we go inside.

* * *

So, it was because of the children.

Corentin turned his head and saw Mathilde on the doorstep, banishing her anger and fear, and she nodded in turn, her gaze riveted on the two little strangers, so pale and thin.

He spread his arms.

We don't have much.

But that evening, they shared. That evening would be the finest meal in eighteen years.

The evening that would bring living people back into the world, and other voices, other words—shared memories, which the children listened to, their jaws dropping, unable to understand what they were hearing, laughter, fear, a certain idea about the future. Everyone was heading west. That's the way it had been from the start, but the migration had intensified, because of the ever more numerous, ever more violent groups that were spreading terror in the South and the East, plundering everything in their path. They'd formed a community, they were crazy, they came to steal and kill and knew nothing else.

This group, the nine of them, had managed to slip through their fingers. A few weeks earlier, there had been fourteen of them. That was why they left. That was why they too were heading west. They shook their heads, they didn't want to talk about it. Not in front of the children. Not to relive those terrible hours. Mathilde and Corentin didn't ask any questions. They could imagine, they didn't need words. These lives so rare they had become infinitely precious; these lives worth more than gold—and yet there were others who took them as if they were worth less than nothing. Negligible quantities. Useless presences.

A silence fell around the table.

So, they talked about other things. Forced themselves to. Even if it was still there, somewhere in their minds, they managed to laugh again, and tell old stories. They knew they mustn't obsess about that sort of thing, unless they wanted to give up for good.

Their guests didn't finish everything. They said they'd had enough. It was a lie but—Mathilde gave the children seconds.

After dinner, they put the younger children to bed. Only the adults were left at the table. Corentin poured little glasses of alcohol: this meant a celebration, but also that serious things were preying on his mind, and that they would get there. While the Calvados burned their throats, he ran his finger over the table, looking thoughtful. Then he raised his head and whispered: Now, you have to tell us.

* * *

And what had become of man, to such a point that, in a world where almost everything had disappeared, he remained determined to destroy his fellows one by one, to rob and kill them? At first, Corentin thought the others had to be lying, it was so excessive. He could see the same doubt on Mathilde's face—then he remembered that, a long time ago, the survivors of Nazi concentration camps had also been suspected of lying and making things up, because what they were testifying to was beyond anything anyone could accept, beyond barbarity and cruelty, and no one could hear it and believe it had happened.

At the table, the women trembled, their cheeks streaming with tears. They clenched their fists, not to make any noise, not to let their fear surface suddenly. Mathilde put her hand on theirs.

And they knew it was all true.

They listened to the stories of predation—little groups that had miraculously survived and then were robbed, raped and murdered. Men and women who had made immense efforts to go on living after the catastrophe, and whom one chance encounter had swept aside with the thrust of a knife or the blow of an ax, once they'd been stripped of all their meager belongings and clothing, once they'd been touched and fondled and abused—men, women and children, no one had been spared. Their throats were cut, they were mutilated, eviscerated, hanged.

The ones who had managed to flee would never forget the cries, the violated bodies, everything turned to meat and strips of flesh, pieces of meat, and the fires lit by those savage hordes, the smell of burning everywhere.

But, murmured Corentin, given how few of us there still are on the planet, wouldn't it be better to group together and become allies rather than go killing each other?

No one knew why those people went around killing. They'd lost their minds, only death still flowed in their veins.

And the group of nine survivors had also met people, before and after, who'd managed to get away as well. In every gaze, the same fidgeting of horror and panic, altering their pupils, leaving them hoarse, incapable of saying what they had seen. It was like returning from a war, when images persist on people's retinas, when fear can no longer be made to sleep. It would never be erased. All of them had lost the very things that kept them alive—their last kin, their last blood, the ultimate, fragile conviction that there was something to be hoped for in the world. They had seen their fathers and mothers, brothers and sisters, wives and children, transformed into unspeakable beings, things that were no longer human, either in body or mind—fragments, shreds, laments, savage methodical destruction, a nameless crushing—and suddenly Mathilde, her face gone pale, her fingers clinging to her dress, said to them: Please, no more.

T he nine survivors left the next morning. Once they had gone around the second bend, Mathilde turned to Corentin.

They'll find us, too, she declared.

She didn't need to say who would find them. He nodded. She gripped his arm, an unbelievable strength in her hands.

Corentin, this time you must believe me when I tell you we have to leave.

And he closed his eyes and murmured, Yes.

* * *

And nothing in the world had changed between that day and the day before, only the visit of the nine survivors and the words they had said late that night, their fingers clenched around their glasses of alcohol; but everything had changed. Mathilde and Corentin were filled with a sort of urgency. They could sense a drifting danger; they kept watch on the little road leading to the house and listened to the sky.

The time had come.

They gave themselves two weeks.

Two weeks to harvest, too early, the potatoes that would allow them to make it through the trip, because they didn't know how long they'd be walking, they didn't know where the West was.

Two weeks to get ready to leave everything behind, to abandon everything.

They were lucky they'd been warned. They wouldn't be fleeing in a disorderly rush. They could plan: the cart, their belongings, all their meager treasures, the food to start with, three hundred pounds of nearly-ripe potatoes.

For a moment, Corentin gazed at the house, the garden, the pens. The pile of wood stacked to one side, the stockade, the reserves of water, and the little barn that contained almost nothing anymore, and it seemed to him, the time it took to have a quick look around, to be a sort of paradise he had never viewed as one.

But now that they had to leave everything . . .

It all seemed so nicely arranged. So—he hunted for the word—*familiar.*

He could understand why some people who are threatened by hurricanes or tidal waves refuse to leave their homes.

Once again, it would be heartbreaking. It would never stop.

Mathilde came and placed her hand gently on his shoulder. She said nothing. He lowered his head and smiled.

Mathilde—he didn't know what they meant to each other, eighteen years on. They lived like animals, driven by the sole desire to survive: to eat and drink, to reproduce. To find a way to keep on going, while the years went by, even if it meant privation, discomfort, the absence of any future. And more than once both of them, surely, had hoped for death, because it was too hard to keep on going in this world, too much effort. But strength was on the side of instinct, it wasn't deliberate. Life had preserved them.

Mathilde—had she forgiven him, they'd never spoken of it, they never spoke of anything other than everyday priorities. For years she'd hated him, he was sure of it. And then something had gradually waned, grown softer, maybe after the birth of Sirius. Mathilde loved her children more than anything, and love had prevailed over everything else. For a long time, Corentin had kept out of her way. He, too, had found sustenance in his children, in their unfathomable lightness, their undiluted joy. He had watched all six of them grow up without bitterness or regret, taking life as it was given to them, neither ugly nor beautiful—just as it was.

But between the two of them, Mathilde and Corentin, was there room for love? She hadn't chosen him; he'd desired her because there was no one but her. What example had they set for the children—never holding hands, never kissing, what were they saying about themselves, their indifferent gazes always looking elsewhere.

And yet, I love her, he thought, and he placed his hand on Mathilde's, where she was still holding his shoulder.

Then he thought he was reasoning as if he were about to die. Like a very old man.

And was suddenly afraid this might be a premonition, but it couldn't be, he still had to lead them, Mathilde and the six children, and the dogs, they had to leave, go on the journey, without him they wouldn't make it. He shook his head, brusquely. Mathilde let her hand slide down his back, then withdrew it.

They had two weeks left.

Two weeks that would be incomprehensibly sweet, while at the same time, every day would go by too slowly, with the fear that something might happen before they left, two weeks was nothing compared to the eighteen years they had just endured, deep in the valley, but it was as if time were suddenly accelerating, as if things were hurtling forward.

And yet again, it was all in their minds.

But it was true, too.

* * *

They had to explain to the children.

Leave: an unknown word. The youngest ones began crying.

Elsewhere. They didn't know what *elsewhere* meant. They didn't even know it existed. In spite of Mathilde's lessons, the map of the world had remained completely abstract, they thought it was a drawing, a legend, anything but real.

And, terrified at the thought they would have to leave the only place they knew, they implored; Corentin looked at them and thought they were like people from long ago who believed that you fell off the edge of the horizon because the earth was flat; that's what they were like, his six sons and daughters, little children who didn't know anything, had no experience, didn't want to change, even what was worst. And he, Corentin, bore most of the blame, he was the one who'd drawn a circle on the hiking map, who'd set the bounds of the universe that they'd become sated with, that they'd explored for eighteen years without ever going beyond the thick black line on the paper; beyond it lay the unknown, and no one could say what they would find there.

There it was, maybe they would fall off into the void.

Corentin's heart sank. They were so fragile, his children, his survivors—because that was truly what they were. So weak and helpless, like fireflies shining in the night, and all it would take was a puff of air to terrify them, snuff them out. Corentin wanted to take them into his arms, all of them at the same time, to reassure them, and he would have to find the words, but he didn't, he went from one to the other, and kissed them, in silence, held them tight, one by one, for a long time.

Only the eldest, Altair and Electra, and Sirius, had shining eyes. Not with tears: it was fervor, a fierce joy, fear outflanked by the excitement of this departure, which they awaited as if paradise lay at the other end; leaving was both terrible and magical at the same time, and the younger children gazed at them, stunned, when they said: we can't wait.

* * *

Bit by bit, from exultation or fear, they relaxed.

They wanted to know.

They asked—elsewhere.

Where is it? How long does it take to get there? Will there be gardens, and streams, and big black forests? Will there be dogs? Will we find the two children who slept here two nights ago?

Mathilde answered their questions as if it was a game. She was careful not to make anything sound too wonderful, not to disappoint them. They got all worked up, they imagined all sorts of things, since they didn't know anything. She tried to restrain their flights of fancy. No one could say for sure what they would find in the West. But maybe yes, maybe it would be their salvation. And in any event, they had to go there— and then the memory of the stories the nine survivors had told came back to her, and she got a nervous tic on her face, she pretended it was nothing, she let them ramble, wander to the edge of their imaginary worlds, both so new and so limited.

She thought: this tiny world. These tiny children.

W as it a wise choice to wait? Corentin shared his doubts with Mathilde. She put her hand on his arm. It would take them weeks to get to the West. They needed food. What was he afraid of, basically—he himself didn't know, it was something fleeting, an impression, a premonition, just like the feeling of fragility that had overcome him, suddenly getting old, the fatigue he could not shake, and which left him feeling drained already first thing in the morning.

But once again, he could not die now.

And it was the clouds, too, that had changed color, the air bringing a new chill, the dogs' howling at night, whimpering in a different way. So many little signs he noticed and that meant nothing, it was just his own fear that was skewing his gaze, he slapped his fears onto the world and the world was still just as deserted, just as smooth as it had been for eighteen years.

But he couldn't convince himself of this altogether.

And he couldn't speak about it to Mathilde, either, she'd dismissed him, pushed him away, the first time he brought it up—You'll bring us bad luck.

He kept looking for clues, changes, smells.

It smells of death, he thought.

And immediately afterwards: shut up, shut up. It's in your head, you're sick.

Sick.

Mathilde said that, too.

But maybe she was the one who couldn't see.

* * *

After ten days had gone by, Corentin dug up a potato plant. He knew it was too soon, but only a few days too soon, next to nothing. The tubers would not grow that much more if they left them for one more week. The children were sick of waiting, even if no one said so. They had their sights on the second day before departure—because on the second day before, they'd open their mouths, start asking questions, share their nervousness, it would all spill out, all at once, their hands trembling again when the time came to start wrapping things up for good, and alarm bells would start going off in their heads.

So maybe cutting it all short, bringing everything forward five or six days would be the solution. Take them by surprise. Not leave them any time to ruminate before the countdown.

Now, thought Corentin.

He dug up the first clump of earth, and the children ran over with buckets to fill them with potatoes.

They still look good, said Perseus, in his clear voice.

It was not entirely true. But it didn't matter.

This time, they wouldn't be able to let them dry on the ground. Altair and Sirius took the other spades. Mathilde, Electra, Garnet, Urania, and Perseus: they brushed the tubers, lowered them delicately into the buckets which they would then empty into the cart. It took them all afternoon. And like before—effort repelled fear, they began laughing and singing, even though they were tired, because they knew there'd be a feast that night, on potato harvest day they didn't have to watch their appetite, and they could all eat their fill.

They scurried around the garden like ants, the youngest carrying buckets that were too heavy for them, the older children breathing heavily over their spades, they took turns, sat on the ground to catch their breath, excited in advance at the thought of a feast, of abundance.

That's the way it had always been.

Harvest day had always been a feast day. The only one they knew. It was Christmas, Easter, and birthdays all rolled into one, all those words that didn't mean much anymore, something shining in their eyes, a wonderful fragrance, they wouldn't have missed it for the world.

A feast!

Mathilde had added sausages from a can, rinsing off the sauce, and cooking them for hours to make sure they wouldn't get sick, there was a smell of boiled meat—and they let out cries of joy. She opened a bottle of old cider, and, of course, it was insipid and tasted of cork, but Corentin explained to the children once again what alcohol was, what a drunk man was, and they all got drunk, they were all convinced they'd drunk too much, that it was too strong, they said silly things, and couldn't stop laughing. The three youngest fell asleep at the table. The older ones carried them up to their mattresses.

And Corentin, a bit later, lying down beside Mathilde, thought how lucky they were, fate would not destroy such a lovely family, destiny—it had to—had feelings, would show mercy, take pity on them.

The dark omens inside him had vanished. He took this as a sign.

It had passed them by.

Or was so close that there was nothing to be done, nothing to hope for—but Corentin didn't think about that.

The next day, the children looked at the sheet of paper pinned on the wall. The calendar Corentin had sketched out was no longer valid, they'd dug up the potatoes ahead of time and the days had taken a sudden leap forward.

When are we leaving, they asked worriedly.

Today.

They burst out laughing, as if it were impossible.

Today!

Corentin spread his arms, and they gathered in the circle of his embrace.

At noon.

He thought: for the angelus.

* * *

The potatoes and their belongings were piled in the cart. It will be heavy, thought Mathilde, looking at the overflowing cart, and yes it was so small, but it contained their entire lives. And it was incredible that their lives could fit into such a ridiculously small space, incredible and terrifying, eight lives reduced to what was little more than a big wooden chest; they had no choice, nor did they have anything else to fill it any further, and perhaps that was the most disconcerting thing of all, that they had nothing to take with them.

Clothing, blankets, food and water.

The odd memento—a piece of sculpted wood, a shiny pebble, objects the children had made of clay and which they would eventually leave behind because they were pointless, it would be hard enough to push the cart up the valley, every fraction of a pound mattered now.

The dogs were in the pens; they'd set them free at the last minute.

Corentin put things in, took them out, piled them up.

He, too, thought the cart seemed tiny. But his gaze was practical: too much weight, not enough room; he knew that Garnet, Urania and Perseus would need to sit there in order to rest, they didn't have the strength or the stamina to walk for hours on end in the cold and drizzle, they wouldn't be able to make it through the long days. So, he had to push the potatoes further back and fashion a bench where the children could rest and fill every last empty space, while making sure everything remained accessible for when Mathilde, in the evening, would ask for a pan, a blanket, or a knife.

He'd readied the tarps and wooden stakes to attach to the cart for a covering in the evening, like a tent; he didn't know if it would be enough to protect them from the wind and rain. They'd go past dozens, hundreds of houses on their way, where they could take shelter if they couldn't stand the discomfort of the outdoors anymore; but there would be the remains of bodies, which wouldn't have decomposed in eighteen years—hair and bones—and he couldn't see them clearing the rooms every evening, maybe the barns would be okay; he'd warned the children.

There would be dead people on their way, dead people were nothing to worry about.

The three eldest, who'd been with him several times to the Little Town, they remembered. The three youngest had never seen any corpses. The prospect filled them with excitement.

When are we leaving?

In two hours.

What's an hour?

Corentin said, instead:

Soon.

Perseus blocked off a space between his hands.

Soon, like this?

Corentin harnessed himself to the cart. He had reinforced the harness with ropes and old leather belts; it was the harness he'd used in the early years, when he used to go emptying the town of supplies. The minute he put the straps over his shoulders, the feeling came back to him—the pain, the tiredness, the necessity.

He needed Altair, Sirius and Electra's help to get the overloaded cart moving. Even though he'd made sure everything was equally distributed, it still weighed far too much. Everything crushed him into the ground already, into the blacktop which had disintegrated into a scree of uneven fragments. He could feel his legs wobbling with each forward step, as if he were climbing a stairway with a metal beam in his arms.

How much, he wondered with despair. Four, five hundred pounds?

And who would help him go uphill?

And who would help restrain it, going downhill?

Every instant of every day.

It would take them years to get there.

Mathilde saw the expression on Corentin's face.

She understood at once.

It was like an electric shock in her gut.

There was just one word, which she uttered in silence, and he read it on her lips.

No.

A prayer.

No, we cannot stay. We have to go. You have to find a solution. We are running out of time.

Madness: let's leave everything. Take nothing with us and go. We'll run. We'll fly.

All of this in her clear blue eyes, in her silent voice, tossed right in his face.

It brought tears of rage and disappointment to his eyes. He couldn't pull the cart. They wouldn't manage.

They needed it.

So, he emptied it.

He left half the potatoes next to the house. It was wrenching. What he was leaving there might be what they needed to finish their journey. So much effort. So much hope.

That was the world from before, that was Augustine, eighteen years blasted to smithereens.

He kept the bare minimum so that the cart was light enough for him pull it on his own—or Altair, who wanted to try, or Sirius.

On the path there was a strange pile of odds and ends and potatoes.

Cook them, said Corentin to Mathilde, pointing to the tubers, his voice deep with weariness.

Cook them, so that at least we can enjoy them.

Let's eat as many as we can.

Enough to make ourselves sick.

Put them in our pockets, keep them in our mouths, take them in our hands. Stuff ourselves full of them, because there'll be too many—never once in eighteen years has there been too much food.

We'll have another feast, a feast of wasting and throwing away.

It will taste bitter, this one.

But let's do it.
Afterwards, we'll get going.
It will be noon by then.

But they didn't get as far as noon.
Time stopped before that.

T hey came without anyone hearing.

They came, and it was a little before the angelus, which hadn't rung in eighteen years.

The dogs sensed them first and began barking behind the stockade. Blind Boy, at the door to the house, had frozen. Corentin, Mathilde, and the children: they were outside the house, eating the potatoes, trying to find a moment of joy. They were only half listening—the dogs often whined, there was nothing to be done, the moment they were put in the pens they started barking.

Corentin shouted at them. They didn't stop barking. So, he frowned. He took the gun which, as always, was leaning against the wall. As a precaution. The children, who were talking among themselves, saw what he did, and froze.

What.

He shrugged.

Because of the dogs.

Blind Boy strained toward the top of the valley, toward the old cracked road.

For a moment, Corentin thought of ordering the children inside. He refrained. Mathilde had already told him off for his unhealthy vigilance. How many times had he made them go inside, barricade themselves—for nothing.

Fear was taking root, and he was transmitting it to them.

Said Mathilde.

That was why he stayed silent.

That was why, despite the dogs and his concern.

Their chatter became hesitant, then slowly resumed. Corentin was still standing in the middle of the path. They were a few yards from each other; he was in front. Instinctively. The children weren't paying attention to him anymore. Feeling alarmed, giving a start: they knew it all by heart.

Then Blind Boy growled, and Corentin's heart leapt in his chest.

Blind Boy growled—it was already too late.

* * *

They filled the entire path. The moment they arrived, these people who had been so silent up to then, they burst out laughing. Thundering laughter, aggressive and nasty. Huge. The laughter of thirty hirsute human beings, and Corentin took a step back. He had forgotten it was possible to be so many.

He cocked the rifle. The metallic sound brought them all to a halt.

Mathilde and the children were on their feet. Motionless.

The group facing them: motionless, too. All eyes on Corentin—and the rifle.

Corentin could feel himself trembling. Could feel his legs wanting to sit down, his breath ragged, uneven. Behind the house, the dogs' howling made it impossible to think.

Howling, and fear. A fucking huge fear, because he instantly understood that these humans hadn't come to beg: they had come to take by force.

But he said it anyway.

To make sure, or to gain some time.

He said: What do you want?

A thick bearded man, all in black, stepped forward and spread his arms.

Everything!

The roar of his voice split the air. And once again, the others burst out laughing, cried out, their arms raised and fists clenched.

And Corentin knew it to his core: it was true. They would take everything.

He glanced, terrified, at Mathilde—they would take her. And at his children; they would take them, too, already their gazes were coveting shamelessly. There were women in the group, too, and Corentin hoped they might intervene, he prayed that this stupid idea—that some remnant of kindness might temper the others, the brutes, the beasts—those were the words knocking in his head.

But the women were nothing like that. Corentin's gaze swept over the thirty figures, he heard the slurs coming as often from the mouths of the women as from the men, and he was convinced there was no pity or kindness to be found in any of them: they marched together, they robbed and killed together.

So, there was silence.

Corentin did not hope they would hesitate; but the rifle worried them. They didn't have one. In eighteen years, after so much violence, they had used up all their ammunition, and they'd thrown out their useless weapons. And in their furious gazes, the questions kept coming: was the rifle loaded, would Corentin dare to shoot, how many bullets.

Seven, thought Corentin, paralyzed over his weapon.

Seven bullets right there, under his hand. He had fifty or so in reserve, in the house. Out of reach. And in any case, he would never have time to reload.

The others were eyeing the rifle, all they could do not to grab it. They wanted it.

They don't have one, thought Corentin again.

But they had metal bars in their hands. They had knives as long as their arms, sabers, the blades of cutthroats.

What use was he, standing there with his rifle facing thirty psychos with their lethal weapons? What would happen once he'd shot seven of them?

He was panicking, his thoughts slamming together, disordered. He had to do something, otherwise he'd end up incapable of doing anything. But what would be the point? Where would it lead? He felt horribly alone. No one could help him. He knew that time was against him—he looked like an indecisive coward; facing him, right there, they would soon march on him. They would take the rifle from his hands without a struggle, without a fight, without courage, all they had to do was pry his fingers apart, one by one.

He couldn't think straight.

Then suddenly, he knew.

The shock of it almost made him stumble. He leaned forward slightly to weather the blow, it was only in his head, and it was terrifying. But absolutely certain.

He had to kill the children.

His children.

It was the only way to prevent them from being raped, tortured, or taken away as slaves—slain on the spot if they tried to resist.

Kill his children. His eyes filled with tears. He couldn't. It was beyond him.

But when he saw, again, those avid, dirty, repulsive faces before him. When he saw how they swayed and lurched, impatient to make a move.

Seven cartridges.

Six children.

And Mathilde.

Mathilde who was looking at him, her eyes bulging. Mathilde who had understood when he did. Who, just as the tears began to streak her face, gave a tiny little sign with her head.

Yes, she said.

Kill us. Don't leave us.

Oh, God.

Sacrifice them. There was no other way out.

As for himself, he didn't care. It didn't even occur to him to think about himself. He would be slaughtered during the attack. It was not important. He had to die. He could not stand to be the only survivor.

A few feet away, the group was grumbling.

Altair had been holding Blind Boy from the beginning.

Hold him, shouted Corentin. Don't ever let him go.

To contain the hatred, to not start the war.

Behind them, the dogs went on baying, he could hear them leaping against the stockade, as if they too had sensed that the humans who'd come were nothing but anger and barbarity.

Now it was urgent. Tearfully, he thought—Quick, quick.

His hands trembling on the butt of the rifle.

He had to kill the girls first. In case he didn't have time for everything. They'd be made to suffer the worst.

Electra, Garnet, Urania.

A sob welling in his throat.

Gradually, he turned toward them.

Toward his six children, standing stock still in a line to his right; his angels, his treasures.

Perseus too, among the first—the youngest. Corentin didn't want him to see. Not to live even one moment with a shattered childhood.

There were two left.

Two.

Altair and Sirius: just then, they looked at him. And he knew they had guessed, too. He saw the fear in their eyes—fear, and with a faint nod of their heads, the sign that they accepted.

Flesh of his flesh.

He couldn't wait anymore. Out of the corner of his eye he could sense movement among the group, they were coming imperceptibly closer.

How much left—ten or twelve yards between them.

Altair, Sirius.

And Mathilde.

The pressure made him stagger, he was gasping for air, he felt like he was suffocating.

And then there came a cry.

Papa!

Altair begging him. Altair forcing him.

And so, screaming wildly, an animal cry, Corentin fired.

He shot the seven cartridges, one after the other. Seven bullets, only the clicking of the pump between each one.

It was quick. Six, seven seconds.

No one had the time to do anything.

Seven thunderclaps ringing in his ears like the sound of a cannon.

They fell.

There were shouts. Corentin didn't hear them. He had gone mad.

He could sense movement, yelling, mayhem. He knew he had just brought chaos to the end of the valley—there was no other solution.

And he had hoped for some sort of miracle, and that this would be the end.

But nothing was over.

* * *

In the last instant, he had turned aside.

In the last instant, his courage had failed him. He couldn't do it. He saw his children, ghostly figures, blurry, sublime. It was so unnatural. So inhuman. His entire being rejected it.

So, he had spun around and fired into the mass.

A tight, compact mass.

That would win every time.

Seven corpses that were no longer laughing or jeering.

And he was there with his useless rifle in his open hands, and it fell to the ground, while he stood there, arms dangling, his eyes open wide, stunned and motionless.

He saw the surge. He saw the group rush toward him, when they realized the rifle was empty. Arms outstretched.

There was nothing he could do. He wasn't there anymore. In shock.

And maybe he had time to see the raised knife, maybe he understood, from its trajectory, that it would land in his chest, and go right through him; the gesture had been powerful, enraged—so he didn't move.

He looked. He was beyond all possibility. He couldn't see anymore.

The blood splattered in his eyes.

* * *

Corentin fell backwards and his head hit the ground.

In that moment, his brain began to work again, his thoughts returned to him.

The horror was giving him life. He screamed.

He screamed her name.

Mathilde, Mathilde!

But he knew she was already dead.

He knew that by rushing to stand in front of him, to receive the blade right in her heart, she had taken his place. She had forced his hand. She was giving him a chance to save them—the children.

Their children.

Corentin gave a roar so loud it drowned out the clamor.

He had no illusions, no hope.

It was just to say.

It was for Mathilde.

Next to him, his six children had formed a circle. They had taken up sticks and tools.

There was this gaze they all shared.

Wild. Magical.

They smiled at each other.

The humans were coming toward them, a braying horde they no longer feared.

They gripped their weapons.

Papa.
Papa . . .
It was far, far away.

A murmur. So faint, after the clamor, the chaos, the darkness.

Corentin didn't want to come back.

The voice, very soft, but insistent.

Papa.

A hand on his hand—at least that is what he thought.

He felt as if he were making his way back up through the bowels of a stinking, viscous earth, he was half suffocated, stunned he wasn't completely dead.

Dead—all his consciousness suddenly burst upon him.

He moved his eyebrows. Was that enough? He didn't know.

Dead, but not him. He could hear. There was so much pain in his head and in his body. That wasn't it, being dead.

So many images.

Mathilde's body, collapsing on his, the blood he had thought, at first, was his own, before meeting his wife's gaze—her head flung backward, she was gone already—before he saw the huge wound, and the red streaks on his hands when he tried to staunch the blood.

Those sick humans—who had charged like an absurd battalion, in rows of gray and black, vociferating, their steel blades pointed at them, at Corentin, above all—and suddenly, the last howling.

The dogs.

No one had noticed the mayhem behind the stockade. No one could have guessed—not even them—that the dogs would be strong enough, enraged enough, to knock over the fence, drunk with anger and helplessness, and all of a sudden, they had bolted, a mad onrush, their massive bodies hurtling forward at full speed, their jaws open on their shining fangs, already dazed by the prospect of the kill—and that was the last thing Corentin saw before the blow that had knocked him down: the stampede of the howling pack.

For him, time had stopped there.

A spark of mordant joy.

What happened afterwards he didn't know. He'd lost consciousness. He'd hoped that he and his children would be torn to shreds, that the madness would overcome both sides and leave no survivors. He remembered feeling a flow of air as the enraged dogs passed over his body.

And then nothing.

The fact that Altair and Sirius had joined the pack, crushing the skulls of the attackers with their crowbars: this he didn't see. The fact that Electra, hearing her brother's cry, rounded up the younger children to seek shelter in the house: he didn't see that, either. Nor did he witness the fury of the dogs as they surrounded his sons to protect them, nor the exalted fear of the younger children who, once they were in the hidden recesses of the attic upstairs, had found makeshift weapons—if it came to that, if they had to save their skin.

He had missed all that. He'd been spared that terror.

His children, fighting a war.

Then he opened his eyes, and his head was pounding, he felt nauseous.

He opened his eyes, he was lying on the ground.

A strange vision, from ground level. For a moment he wondered where he was. Motionless bodies were scattered all around him. Men and dogs. He clenched his hand on the pebbles, he had to get up. Sit up.

Papa.

Who is it?

It's me.

You—he gave a faint smile.

All evening long he didn't move. He didn't want help. Twice he had thrown up, he wasn't hungry. All they could do was look after him. They brought blankets out, made a fire. He didn't eat anything. He kept his eyes open on this deep stupor that wouldn't leave him.

They dragged the corpses further away and covered them with tarps.

They buried the dogs. Corentin heard them sobbing. Mathilde's body—they'd already carried it to the end of the garden, wrapped in a long blue sheet; they'd laid her gently next to a flower that had sprouted out of nowhere, and then they left her, they felt too much sorrow, they'd go back later, they had to see to their father.

They didn't want to leave him on his own, outside. They wrapped him up in blankets, put wood back on the fire. They took turns kneeling by his side, gently placing a hand on his shoulder or his arm.

We're here.

During the night, was it the chill—he slowly sat up, his head not quite as painful. He still felt like throwing up; he took great lungfuls of air and shivered.

Gradually his eyes grew used to the night, to the shock.

He thought he couldn't feel anything anymore, but when he saw them. All six of them.

God, they were there, all six of them.

Closing his eyes for a moment, he uttered their names in

silence. Altair, Electra, Sirius, Garnet, Urania, Perseus. His children.

It brought no solace for the death of Mathilde, who had hollowed out the place she would occupy inside him until his dying day; but a ray of joy he had not seen coming went straight through him. Like a current, a life force. It was an enchantment, incredulous happiness, a hallucination that was no hallucination; a miracle. They were there.

Asleep.

Except for Sirius, who was keeping watch, they must be taking turns. His son was sitting with the rifle across his legs. And Corentin thought—they know how to load it. They know where the bullets are.

He took another breath. A strange peacefulness hung in the air.

Even the dogs were asleep, the ones that had survived. Corentin counted seven. The dogs that had saved them, and he had the answer to his question, he understood why, when at the time it made no sense at all, he had kept them, had fed them.

And Blind Boy?

Sirius turned his head. It was only a murmur but—he looked at his father, went closer not to wake the others.

Blind Boy died.

And the attackers?

They died too, or ran away.

There was a silence.

There's one Blind Boy left, whispered Sirius. A young one.

For a long while Corentin said nothing. Then he nodded.

That's good.

They left the next day.

They buried Mathilde in the garden, where the earth had recovered, at the foot of the two apple trees.

They buried her and they left.

It was over.

Now it was their turn to head west. They wouldn't stop until they got there.

They walked seven abreast along the road, with the dogs weaving in and out of their legs, going on ahead, circling back—dogs playing.

The six children held hands. Sometimes they sang. On uphill stretches, they would push the cart; their cheeks turned pink. They tried to imagine what they would look like, the flowers Corentin had told them about, and the fruit, the animals, the sun. They were sure that in the West they would find all of that.

And in spite of their sorrow, and their fatigue, they were heading west, and they were singing.